TROUBLE ON THE TOMBIGBEE

Trouble on the Tombigbee

A NOVEL BY

Ted M. Dunagan

Junebug Books

Montgomery Louisville

Junebug Books
105 South Court Street
Montgomery, AL 36104

Library of Congress Cataloging-in-Publication Data available upon request.

ISBN-13: 978-1-58838-270-2 (cloth)
ISBN-10: 1-58838-270-2 (cloth)
ISBN-13: 978-1-60306-085-1 (eBook)
ISBN-10: 1-60306-085-5 (eBook)

Map illustration on pages 8–9 by Linda Aldridge.

Design by Randall Williams

Printed in the United States of America
by Sheridan Books.

For Suzanne and Hardy, for Suzanne and Randall, for Lisa, Brian, and Isla, and for Kathy, Dianne, Annell, Sulynn, Kerry, Patsy, Jennifer, John Boy, Valerie, David, Kathleen, Linda, Renea, Hazel, Sue, Danielle, Ms. Scott, Ken, Steve, and all the others who helped, guided, encouraged and supported me as I stumbled along the literary path.

Contents

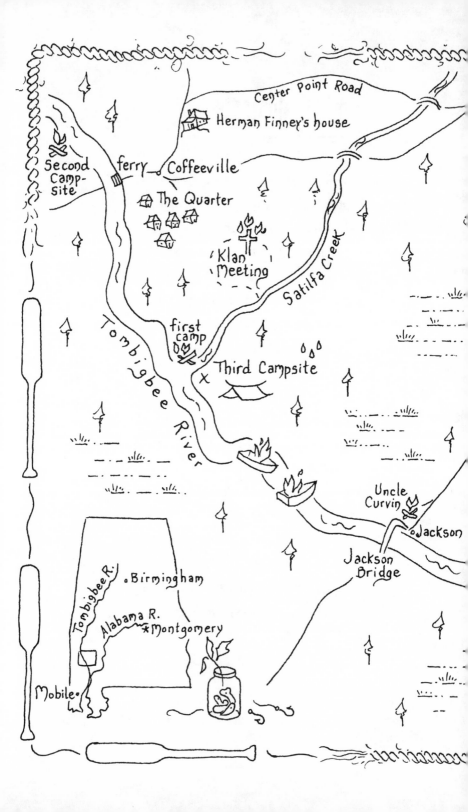

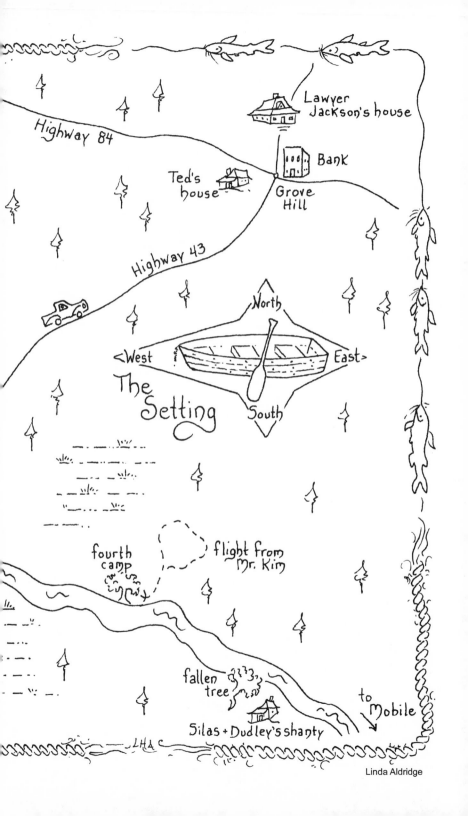

Linda Aldridge

Chapter 1

Walking to the River

The Tombigbee River was an inspiration to both me and my friend Poudlum Robinson, in that it had humble beginnings like us, but went on to be great and mighty. That's what we wanted to do.

I knew a lot about the river because my brother Fred had taught me. It emerged as a tiny stream from springs and marshes in northeastern Mississippi, crossed the state line into Alabama, and by the time it had meandered down to the southwest corner of the state at Coffeeville, it was a wide, deep and imposing body of water, its banks lined with thick hardwood forests.

It continued flowing south for some seventy miles before it merged into the Alabama River and then emptied into the Gulf of Mexico at Mobile.

But the part I was interested in was where the ferry crossed it at Coffeeville. That's where Poudlum and I were heading.

I hadn't seen my friend since January when my family had moved from near Coffeeville to Grove Hill, where I had endured the hardship of adapting to a new school and finding new friends while I missed my old ones. I figured Poudlum was going through some changes, too, because I had read in the newspaper that his school had a new principal who had served in World War II as one of the famous Tuskegee Airmen fighter pilots. The paper had called him Professor Clarence Jamison, and went on to say he expected some of the students at Poudlum's school to follow in his footsteps. Smart as Poudlum was, I figured the professor already had him in his sights.

It was just a few days after I graduated from the seventh grade when word came from Poudlum wanting to know if I was interested in a fishing trip on the Tombigbee. The word came through our old friend, my Uncle Curvin. He was on his way to pick up a load of fertilizer when his old truck came rumbling into my driveway.

As he limped down from the running board, he smiled his toothless smile, looked me up and down and said, "You running up like a weed, son."

"Hey, Uncle Curvin," I said as I grinned back at him.

After we settled down on the front porch, he said, "You ain't home by yourself, are you?"

My momma had given up her milk cow, her chickens, and her garden except for a tiny spot, and had gone to work in a shirt factory, which my daddy called a sweat factory. My oldest brother Ned had gone off and joined the Air Force, and Fred had already landed himself a summer job. So yes, I was home alone, I told him.

"Well, then," he said, "You might be interested in an invite I got for you."

My uncle was always doing that—saying something to

make you curious and then making you drag the details out of him, but today he didn't. I believe it was because he felt sorry for me for being home alone, which there was really no need of because I had discovered the library in Grove Hill and had a stack of books to read, but he didn't know that so he told me right off.

"I was by the Robinsons' place yesterday, and Poudlum wanted to know if you might be interested in a camping and fishing trip down on the river. That boy is growing as fast as you are. And that new professor at his school must be doing something, 'cause Poudlum talks 'bout as good as you do."

Just the mention of Poudlum's name caused memories to wash over me like the spring rains we had been having. Thoughts flashed through my mind of how the two of us had discovered and helped destroy the bootlegger's whiskey still, set our friend Jake on his journey to freedom, been captured by bank robbers, and fished all up and down Satilfa Creek.

"You talking about the Tombigbee River, Uncle Curvin?" I said as my hopes and spirits soared.

"Don't know of no other rivers hereabouts," he said as he loaded his lower lip up with a dip of powdered snuff from a little round metal can.

"When was he talking about going?" I asked breathlessly.

"Whenever you can get yourself down there. Your momma and daddy ought to be home by the time I come back through here with my load of fertilizer. We get it cleared with them, you can go back down to Center Point with me tonight, and you and Poudlum could strike out tomorrow morning."

I think my parents also felt sorry for me for having to stay home alone because they readily allowed me to go off on my great adventure. Even my brother, Fred, after he came dragging home from his job of cutting pulpwood, agreed it was a good idea.

"You and Poudlum done caught all the fish in Satilfa Creek, so I guess the Tombigbee is next," Fred said.

THAT'S HOW POUDLUM AND I ended up walking down Center Point Road toward Coffeeville and the river on a bright and sunny morning in the early summer of 1949.

"How you like living up close to Grove Hill?" Poudlum asked me as we walked along cracking pecans by squeezing two nuts together in a fist.

After Uncle Curvin dropped me off early this morning, Poudlum had doled out two pockets full for each of us while he told me they were last year's crop, and occasionally you would find a bad one, but that most of them were good.

"It's all right," I said as I popped two halves of a tasty nut into my mouth. "But it ain't like living down here."

"How you mean, better or worse?"

"Both, just different. We'll have plenty of time to talk about it on the river. You got any fishing hooks and lines?"

Poudlum produced a flat, red metal Prince Albert tobacco can from his pocket, shook it to make it rattle and said, "Uh-huh, and I got sinkers, too. Mr. Curvin said everything else we gonna need be in the boat."

The boat he was referring to was the one we had found on Satilfa Creek and that our friend Jake had used to go down the creek, cross the river, and escape from Sheriff Elroy Crowe. Jake had said he would leave it on the other side of the river, and Uncle Curvin had recovered it.

"Everything except food," I told Poudlum. "But we'll stop at Robert's Grocery in Coffeeville and buy us some supplies. If we had bought 'em at Miss Lena's Store, we would have had to tote them all the way to the river."

All of a sudden, I noticed Poudlum getting tense, and I looked up and saw we were getting ready to pass where Old Man Cliff Creel had lived before he got hauled off to jail. It had a look of neglect with weeds growing in the flower beds and along the fence. The pasture in the back was empty of any livestock with grass waist-high.

"Has anyone been living here, Poudlum?" I asked in a hushed tone as if danger and evil still lurked about the place.

"Uh-uh, not nobody that anyone has seen. Has you heard anything about that old man?"

Old Man Creel had been the bootlegger whose whiskey still Poudlum had discovered before we and Jake had alerted the revenuers without anyone knowing it was us.

"I just heard he was going to be in jail for a while longer. What do you think happened to that mean dog that chased us up that tree?"

"Jail is a good place for that old man," Poudlum said. "As for that dog, I hear tell his cousin, Mr. Conway Creel, took him. "'Spect we might find out if that's the case since we got to walk right by his house on the way."

"What! Poudlum, I don't want to have another run-in with that dog!"

"Don't worry. I hear they keeps him chained up. Besides, I got something that will take care of that dog."

"What?"

Poudlum pulled a little snuff can out of his pocket, one like my uncle dipped out of, and said, "I filled this snuff can up with hot pepper ground up real fine. It's so hot it'll take yo' breath away if you just get one little whiff of it. I'll sling it in that dog's face if he messes with us, then we'll watch him run off looking for a creek to stick his head in."

"Good Lord, I hope nobody mistakes it for real snuff and takes a dip of it."

"Yeah, it probably be worse on a person than it would a dog, if they got a good snoot of it."

We passed Miss Annie Pearl's house, and it wasn't long before Center Point Road ended when it ran smack into the road leading to Coffeeville. Poudlum and I had walked down a lot of dirt roads together, but this was the first paved road we had ever traveled together. It wasn't hot enough yet to make the asphalt unbearable on our bare feet, so we started out walking down the middle of it.

We hadn't gone far before Poudlum grabbed my arm and said, "Uh oh!"

"What? What is it, Poudlum?"

"That's where Herman Finney lives, up on the left!"

"So? What you worried about that for?"

"He chunks rocks at me sometime when I go by his house."

I knew Herman from when I had gone to school at Coffeeville. He was a grade ahead of me but performed like he was a grade behind. Besides that he was red-headed and had lots of freckles on his face, and he was bigger than us, and I knew he wouldn't hesitate to use his weight to push a smaller kid around. I had seen him do it before, and I knew him for the bully he was.

"Why does he throw rocks at you, Poudlum?"

"'Cause I'm colored—yells a lot of nasty names at me, too."

"And you ain't never done nothing to him?"

"Nary a thing. I just be dodging rocks and running."

"I bet he won't be throwing any rocks at you today."

"Probably won't, 'cause I'm with you, but that don't mean he won't be wanting to."

Herman's front yard was fenced in with wire and littered with two old rusted-out pickup trucks with no wheels on them sitting on wooden blocks. There was a big black and sooty wash pot next to a pile of split fire-wood with empty buckets and jars strewn about like someone had begun several tasks and then left them all unattended to.

We were almost past the place, and I was beginning to hope we would be able to pass without any kind of confrontation with Herman, but then I saw him come around from behind the wood pile where I suspected he had been watching us the whole time.

"Hey, y'all!" he yelled as he began walking toward the fence. I noticed he had one hand full of rocks.

We stood our ground, and I looked him in the eyes at first, then I let my gaze drop to his hand that clutched the rocks. When he saw me looking at his hand, he relaxed his grip, and the rocks trickled down to the ground.

"Hey, Herman," I said.

His eyes darted back and forth between us before he said, "Where y'all think y'all going?"

I deferred to Poudlum, remaining silent as I turned my head to face him. He hesitated for a moment or two before he said, "Why, uh, we is going fishing."

"I didn't ask you, boy!" Herman lashed out. Then he sneered, turned back toward me and said, "How about it? Where ya'll heading to?"

"Fishing, just like Podlum told you," I answered. "Why you got to hear it twice?"

"'Cause you know how they lie. You can't put no truck in nothing they say."

I had had just about enough of Herman. "Poudlum don't lie, Herman, and he's a friend of mine. Now we got to be getting on down the road. We'll see you later," I told him as we turned and started walking away.

"See him a lot later as far as I'm concerned," Poudlum whispered to me.

"Wait a minute," Herman said. "Where did y'all steal them pecans?"

I had kept cracking nuts and popping the meat into my mouth during the entire encounter with Herman. When he said what he said, I almost choked. Then in disbelief I stuttered, "We-we-we didn't steal no pecans, these came from Poudlum's backyard where they fell off the tree!"

"They probably stole the tree," Herman said. "Hey, I might come down to the river later and y'all better not be fishing in my favorite fishing hole!" Herman called out as we walked away from him.

"Don't pay no 'tention to him," I told Poudlum. "Just keep walking."

Just before we rounded a curve in the road. Herman yelled out one last veiled threat. "I bet y'all didn't know my daddy belongs to the Klan!"

"You hear what he said?" Poudlum asked.

"Yeah, I heard. Don't let it bother you 'cause Herman ain't nothing but a bully, and I know how to handle bullies."

We had barely recovered from our run-in with Herman when a new challenge loomed up before us. It was Old Man Creel's cousin's house where that mean bulldog was supposed to be. We cautiously crossed to the other side of the road as we approached it.

"I don't see him. Does you?"

I was too busy looking for a tree to climb to answer Poudlum.

"There he is!" Poudlum hissed. "See over yonder laying in the shade of that mulberry tree. Thank the Lawd, he's chained to it!"

I looked and sure enough there was that dog, the one that had chased Poudlum and me up a tree and held us captive until our friend Jake had come to our rescue. He looked like he was dozing.

"Walk real soft like," Poudlum whispered. "Maybe he won't wake up 'til we gone out of sight."

Too late! That dog's head popped up and he looked straight at us. He sniffed the air a few times, and then to our amazement, he whimpered and retreated behind the trunk of the mulberry tree.

"Why he's acting like he's scared of us," I said.

"Uh-huh, I 'spect that's what it is," Poudlum said. "I think he probably 'members us, and he 'members getting popped in his privates with a rock shot from Jake's slingshot."

"But we didn't do that. Jake did."

"Yes, but if you recollects, Jake made his shot from the woods and that dog never seen him."

It became clear to me after Poudlum said this, that the dog probably associated his pain with us since we were the ones he chased up the tree, and I had taken two fruitless shots at him with my slingshot.

We watched carefully over our shoulders as we walked tentatively on down the road, but the dog never emerged from his sanctuary behind the tree, and Poudlum and I walked on with a sense of satisfaction in that even though he was a dog, we had put one bully in his place.

Just the same, when we came to a stand of hardwoods by the road, we stopped and cut us each a strong hickory stick to walk with.

Nary a vehicle passed us on that lonely road, and we finally rounded the bend and arrived in Coffeeville. My old schoolhouse was over to our left, looking alien without any teachers or kids on the grounds.

A little farther down the road at the corner was Robert's Grocery Store where we rested, had ourselves a NuGrape soda pop and a package of Fig Newtons.

Afterwards, we purchased some canned goods, saltine crackers, and two big slabs of hoop cheese, enough to sustain us for several days.

A LITTLE FARTHER AND the road came to a dead end at Highway 84, where we turned west and headed down the long hill toward the river.

"Wonder where Mr. Curvin left that boat?" Poudlum asked.

"He said he would leave it down there next to the ferry. Said Old Man Henry Williams, who operates the ferry, would watch it for us."

Finally there was the river, wide and deep, and also the ferryboat. It was just a big floating platform that had been operated by Mr. Henry ever since I could remember. Most everyone called him "Mister Henry," both white and colored. I believe it had something to do with his ferry being the only way to get your car or truck across the river.

He would slide two big wide and thick boards from the bank of the river to the ferry and use them to drive vehicles onto the deck when somebody wanted to cross the river over into Choctaw County. He carried them across for fifty cents.

When we walked up, Mr. Henry was working on his little four-cylinder motor, which powered his ferryboat. He raised his head up from his task and said, "Hey, boys. "'Spect y'all be looking for that boat Mr. Curvin left here for y'all."

"Yes, suh," Poudlum told him.

"Well, it's right down yonder," he said as he pointed a few yards below the ferry. "Right where I helped him unload it early dis morning. Said you boys would be along directly and planned to spend a few days fishing on de river."

"That's right, Mr. Henry," I told him as we turned toward the boat.

"Well, lookahere, you boys need to be real careful out on that old river."

Before I had moved to Coffeevilee, Poudlum and I had been going over to the spot on Satilfa Creek about twice a week, where the moonshine still had been, and I had taught him to swim. He had become a real good swimmer, too, just like I knew he would. So I told Mr. Henry, "We can both swim, and we're not afraid of the river."

"Ain't the river you got to worry about so much," he said with an ominous sound to his voice. "It's some of the folks you run into on the river."

Chapter 2

The Mouth of the Satilfa

"What you 'spect he meant by that?" Poudlum asked as we walked down toward the boat.

"Shoot, I don't know, but from the way he said it I 'spect we ought to pay some heed to him."

"I wish we had got up early this morning and rode in with Mr. Curvin. We done that, we probably would've already had us a mess of catfish."

"You probably right about that, but I don't like getting up before daylight."

"What yo' uncle went over the river for so early this morning?"

"Said he was going over to Choctaw County and do some horse trading."

"He gonna get hisself a hoss?"

"I don't think so. What I think is that 'horse trading' is a couple of words that don't really mean what they say."

"What they mean then?"

"I believe they mean being real careful and making sure you get a good deal when you're doing business with someone."

We were almost to the boat when Poudlum said, "Where you think we ought to set up our campsite?"

"I don't know. Just down the river a little ways I guess."

"I think we ought to cross the river and make camp over there."

"How come?"

"'Cause if we stays over on this side Herman Finney might come down here and be pestering us."

"I 'spect you might be right about that, Poudlum."

When we got to the boat we saw a big brown mound in the middle of it, and it turned out to be a tarp my uncle had used to cover up the stuff in the boat.

As we removed it, I told Poudlum, "Uncle Curvin said we could use this tarp to make us a tent or a lean-to if it rains. Let's fold it up and stow it under one of the seats."

Once we did that, we discovered my uncle had left some treasures for us in the boat. There were several cane fishing poles, a little box with hooks, lines, sinkers, and corks, a black iron skillet, blankets, wooden matches in a waterproof bag, a big bucket, and an ax.

But Poudlum discovered the most important item and called out, "Hey, Ted! Come look at this!"

I walked down to his end of the boat as he pulled out two quart fruit jars with bright gold caps and filled with a green, yellow, and black mixture of something.

"Look!" he said as he held up one of the jars. "It's catalpa worms, just about the best fish bait in the world!"

Sure enough it was. I took one of the jars and began to examine it. Little air holes were poked into the caps of the jar, and it was full of catalpa worms and leaves from the tree for them to feed on. Those fat fish-catching worms were crawling around inside the jar munching on leaves, not knowing they would soon be taking a perilous swim in the river.

The worms were picked off the tree leaves this time of the year, and I never particularly liked the job of collecting them because they would cling to the leaf with all their little tiny suction-cup legs and spit green juice on your fingers when you tore them loose from the leaves. But it was worth it because catfish loved catalpa worms more than a possum loves a sweet potato.

The catalpa tree is ornamental with showy flowers, but once a year the tree becomes occupied by the pale yellow worms with black heads and black markings. Catfish would jump on these worms like a dog would a bone.

We stowed the worms and our sacks of food in the boat and waved goodbye to Mr. Henry after we pushed off.

As we were paddling toward the other side of the river, Poudlum said, "You think we ought to go upriver or down it?"

"Why don't we do both," I answered.

"How in the world we gonna do that?"

"Easy. We'll go down the river today, and tomorrow we'll go up it."

"Sounds like a good plan to me," Poudlum said. "But I think we ought to take all our stuff with us in case we decide to camp somewhere else instead of coming back here and camping near the ferry."

The boat, eleven feet long and five feet wide, was constructed of thick cypress boards with tar in all the joints and cracks. We had the hang of handling the paddles by the time we reached the middle of the river.

We pulled our paddles in and rigged up four fishing poles. We held two with our hands and tied the other two down and started floating down the river, letting the slow current take us with it. A mighty feeling of just being swept over me, like I was the center of the world, no, the universe.

After a while I looked down toward Poudlum's end of the boat, and from the peaceful way he grinned at me, I knew he felt the same.

In spite of our tried-and-true bait, the fish weren't biting. We drifted about an hour with nary a nibble.

When Poudlum began pulling in the poles, I looked up and asked him what he was doing.

"It's the wrong time of the day for fishing. We gots to wait until shadows start to fall on the water."

"So what you think we ought to do?"

He turned toward the afternoon sun, shaded his eyes against it with his hand, and said, "It's probably nigh on to three o'clock. I figure if we just paddle downriver for a good while we ought to come to the mouth of Satilfa Creek. I hear tell there is some mighty good fishing at that spot, and the light ought to be right about then."

I looked back up the river and figured there was no way we could get lost because the river flowed from north to south, so I agreed with Poudlum, pulled my pole in and grabbed a paddle.

It didn't take us as long as we had anticipated. We hugged

the east side of the river and in about twenty minutes we saw a broad opening in the thick tree line where the color of the water turned from brown to dark green.

"I believe that's it!" Poudlum said excitedly. "Now we gonna catch us some big ones!"

As we guided the boat into the mouth of the creek, Poudlum said, "Whoopee! Look at this place!"

We had entered a cathedral of nature with the ceiling being the limbs of trees reaching out to touch the ones from the opposite side of the creek. The ones that hadn't quite made it were joined by thick muscadine vines forming a leafy dome above the wide mouth of the creek. After we were a few yards in, it seemed as if we were in a floating cave.

We nosed the boat toward a large tree branch which jutted out from the north bank. When we got within reach, Poudlum scrambled to the front of the boat and looped our rope over it.

"This old rope is the same one that was in this boat when we first found it. It looks like it's 'bout half rotten. Hope it holds."

It did, and we sat about baiting our hooks.

As soon as our corks were bobbing in the water, Poudlum said, "You know why I wanted to come down here on the river instead of us going back to the Cypress Hole?"

"How come."

"'Cause they is some whoppers down here in this river, and I aims to catch me one. How come you think catfish love catalpa worms so much?" Poudlum asked as he unscrewed the lid of the jar and extracted a fresh worm.

"I don't know," I told him. "I guess it's just some kind

of secret of nature, kind of like why you and me like pork chops so much."

Poudlum paused, thought for a few moments before he said, "No, I don't believe that's the answer, 'cause when I eat a pork chop it comes out of a skillet and there ain't no hook in it to catch me with."

I considered what Poudlum had said and surmised he was correct, so I just said, "Then I reckon I just ain't go no idea why then."

My honesty seemed to satisfy him, but then he came up with the same question he had asked me one time up on the Cypress Hole.

With a squirming worm between two fingers and a shiny steel fishing hook poised in his other hand he said, "Do you think it's gonna hurt this worm when I stick him with this fishing hook?"

"Naw, they can't feel nothing."

"Then maybe you can tell me why he's going into such a fit of jerking and squirming?" Poudlum said as he skewered the fat worm with his hook.

"I don't know. Just toss him in the water and let's see if they biting yet."

"I'm fixin' to do just that," he said as he adjusted his cork. "Gonna fish a little bit more shallow, too."

My line was already in the water, which was a prettier color than out in the river, but you still couldn't see anything below the murky surface.

What I could see was the floating cork attached to my fishing line dancing on the ripples of the water. My favorite thing to see was when that cork would disappear into the watery world hidden from above. That's when you knew a big channel cat had gone for your bait and gotten his gristly lip hooked on a sharp steel hook with a barb on it so he couldn't slip off.

That's exactly what happened next, but it was Poudlum's cork rather than mine.

"Uh oh!" Poudlum cried out. "It's a big one! I hope he don't break my pole!"

It took a while, but he finally wore that fish out and pulled him alongside the boat. I had pulled in my line so I could help him. Poudlum reached into the water, snagged the fish's lip and tossed him on the bottom of the boat, where the fish began flopping all about.

I leaned over the side of the boat with the bucket and scooped up some water to put the fish in, then I held it while Poudlum extracted his hook.

"Watch out for that dorsal fin," he admonished me. "He'll try to stick you with it."

Once we got the fish in the bucket of water, we both leaned over the side and rinsed the smell of fish from our hands. Then we stood and gazed down at the fish swirling around in his new-found prison.

"That's a good two-pounder," Poudlum said with exhilaration. "I bet they is a bunch more where he came from, and I aims to catch 'em."

And catch them he did. I even caught a couple of nice ones myself. Pretty soon there were so many fat catfish in our bucket there was hardly room for them to move.

"This is one mighty fine fishing hole," Poudlum said. "Just look at it. Because of the trees it stays shady all day long."

That's when I realized we had been there for too long. The mouth of the Satilfa had cast a hypnotic spell on us, and we had lost track of time, and that began to bother me a little bit.

"What time do you think it's getting to be, Poudlum?

"Uh, I 'spect it's getting later on in the day."

"Untie us and let's paddle out on the river and see where the sun is."

A few paddle strokes and we were back out on the river and were shocked to see the sun was just before setting.

"I don't think we have enough time to get back up to the ferry before dark," I told Poudlum.

"You probably right," he said. "But they ain't no clouds, and all we got to do is paddle up the river."

"Yeah, that's true, but I don't think I want to be out on this river at night. What if we run into a big log or something?"

"So what you think we ought to do?"

"Maybe we ought to camp here on the creek bank and go back in the morning," I said.

"That's fine with me. In fact I think I'd rather camp here than back up there. Probably be some more good fishing here early in the morning."

"Then we better make haste and find us a camping spot before it gets dark on us."

A few yards past the tree that we had tied up to earlier, we found a little cove in the creek with a sandy beach, which we slid our boat up onto. We used our ax to cut a few small saplings to make a clearing. Then after we unloaded the boat, we placed some of the saplings over our boat so no one would notice it if they came up or down the creek.

"Why you think we need to hide our boat for anyway?" Poudlum asked.

"I don't know, just seems like a good idea, and it gets this brush out of the way. We need to gather us up some wood for our fire while we still got a little light."

Poudlum gazed into the bucket of fish on the ground and said, "If we hadda gone back up to the ferry we could have give some of these fish to somebody. Now what we gonna do with 'em? Sho' can't eat all of 'em."

"We'll just have to throw back the ones we don't eat," I told him.

"That do seem like a shame."

"If we leave them in that bucket of water, they'll sho' die. If we turn them loose, we might be able to catch them again in the morning."

Poudlum gently released the fish one at a time. We watched as they would move slowly at first, then with a dart disappear deep into the water.

As he released the last one, he said to the fish, "Now, don't you go too far 'cause I'll be looking for you in the morning."

Turning back toward me, he said, "I saved this big last one for our supper. I'll dress him if you'll start us a fire."

Poudlum was at the creek's edge giving the fish fillets one last washing, and I was just about to strike a match to light my kindling when I saw his head jerk up suddenly, like he had heard something

Then I heard it, too. It was paddles bumping against the sides of boats, and men's voices. Several of them.

Chapter 3

The Night Hawk

oudlum retreated from the creek bank and stood next to me. We cocked our ears and listened intently, and sure enough the sounds were exactly what we thought they were.

"Who you think that could be?" Poudlum whispered.

"I ain't got the foggiest," I whispered back.

"What you think we ought to do?"

"I think we ought to make sure they don't see us. Quick, let's drag all our stuff into the woods," I said as I scattered my pile of firewood with a swipe of my foot.

The paddle sounds and the voices were coming closer, alerting us that we didn't have much time, so we made haste and by the time the boats came abreast of us we had cleared our campsite and were peeking through heavy foliage at the edge of the creek.

It was dusk but we could still see there were three boats with six men in each one. It wasn't the boats or the men that scared us—it was what they were wearing.

They were all clad in white and had pointed hoods on their heads.

"Lawd have mercy," Poudlum moaned low. "They is the Klan!"

"Hush!" I hissed. "Don't make nary a sound!"

Their faces weren't covered, but there wasn't enough light to recognize anybody. However, the voice of one of them rang out clear over the water when he said, "I smell fish."

"Me, too," another one said. "Supposed to be some mighty fine fishing around here."

"Yeah," the first one said. "But it smells like fresh-caught fish, real strong like."

"Y'all hold it down back there," a voice from the lead boat said. "And get busy paddling because we got about half a mile to go up this creek. And light your lanterns. It's starting to get dark."

I breathed a sigh of relief, and heard Poudlum do the same as the boats moved on past us while they struck matches and lit their lanterns.

Still, we didn't move a hair or make a sound until they were out of sight and out of hearing.

"Whew, Lawdy," Poudlum said as he exhaled heavily. "If them men had a come by five minutes later we would have been frying catfish next to a big fire and probably wouldn't have even heard 'em till it was too late."

"We could have outrun them through the woods," I said.

"Yep, and then we woulda been stuck out in these woods 'side the river all night with nothing to eat."

"Well, the good Lord was looking out for us and they didn't see us."

"They shore did smell our fish though. I had to drop our

supper on the bank when I first heard 'em. Now we gonna be eating cheese and crackers for supper instead of fresh fried catfish, all on account of the Klan."

"Let's get those tree tops off the boat and get moving," I said.

"That sounds good to me. Being out on this river at night don't sound so bad after all."

"We're going up the creek and not out on the river, at least not now," I told Poudlum.

His jaw dropped as he stuttered, "Is-is-is you crazy? Why we want to go up the creek when we know the Klan is messing round up that way?"

"Don't you see? They didn't have their faces covered and they'll have a big fire going and we can sneak up on them and see who they are!"

"You is crazy! What fire you talking about?"

"They not going up the creek to go fishing, Poudlum. You heard one of 'em say they had 'bout half a mile to go. I bet what they doing is having a big Klan meeting and they'll have a big fire going."

"Why you wants to know who they is?"

"Don't you? It's a big deep and dark secret who belongs to the Klan. If you know who they are you'll know who to keep an eye on. If need be you could warn other people about them."

I could see he wasn't convinced, so I went on. "You could figure out a way to warn people without anybody knowing the warning came from you. Besides that, you and me would know something that just about everybody else don't."

I knew Poudlum was with me when I saw his back stiffen. He said, "I 'spect you might be right. It would be some mighty powerful knowledge to know who is in the Klan, more so to me than to you. Let's get our stuff in the boat."

"No, leave everything here for now. We gonna have to move fast to catch them, and maybe even faster when we come back."

"How we gonna see?"

"We'll paddle hard up the middle of the creek till we can catch up close enough to see their lights."

"What if they hear us?"

"Take your knife and cut off a piece of your blanket big enough to wrap around the handle of your paddle, then cut a strip to tie it good. That'll muffle the sound."

"How we gonna see coming back?"

"The *Old Farmer's Almanac* said there's a full moon tonight, so if there's no clouds there'll be plenty of light when it comes up."

"That full moon is probably what got the Klan all stirred up."

We managed to stay in the middle of the creek by watching the fuzzy outlines of the treetops on each bank, and pretty soon we glimpsed lights flickering up ahead.

"See up yonder," Poudlum whispered.

"I see 'em. Now all we got to do is just keep them in sight," I whispered back.

We kept our distance for a while and could hear their voices, but not well enough to distinguish what they were saying. I wanted to get close enough so we could make out exactly what it was they were saying, so I whispered to Poudlum to paddle a little harder.

"What if they sees us?"

"They can't see us. All they'll see is just black night if they look back down the creek. Just keep talking soft so they won't hear us."

Pretty soon we could make out what they were saying. It sounded like the leader again when he said, "There's our signal up ahead. See that light up on the left? That'll be the Night Hawk."

"Who did he say had a light up yonder?" Poudlum whispered.

"He said the 'Night Hawk' or something like that."

"What you 'spect that means?"

"I ain't got the foggiest. Let's get a little closer and see if we can find out."

We got close enough to see they had landed their boats and were all on the bank in a big clearing. We did a few soft backstrokes with our paddles to keep our boat still in the water.

That's when we saw the Night Hawk. He approached the group of men from the boats with his own lantern in his hand. He was dressed in a white robe with a pointy hood, just like them, except he had his face covered with two eyeholes and one for his mouth.

He held up his lantern and said, "You are now entering a secret place among invisible men who relieve the injured and the oppressed and lend succor to the suffering and the unfortunate ones."

"Gentlemen," the leader of the men in the boats said,

"This is the Night Hawk, the officer who will be conducting you through your inductions tonight."

Just about every hair on my young body was stiff with fright when Poudlum said, "Sounds like the Klan gonna get some new members tonight and the Night Hawk is in charge of 'em."

"Yeah, that's what it sounds like to me, too," I told him.

There was enough light and we were close enough now to clearly see the faces of all the men who had arrived in the boats.

"Does you know any of 'em?" Poudlum whispered.

"No. They must all be from over in Choctaw County, but study their faces so we can remember if we see 'em again."

It got real dark and real quiet after they all followed the Night Hawk from the clearing and onto a trail leading into the woods.

"What now?" Poudlum asked. "It's too dark to see much of anything."

"Let's paddle over to the bank and tie the boat up. We'll leave it a few yards down the creek from theirs. That way we'll be below them in case we have to make a run for it."

We gently nosed the boat into the bank. It made a soft brushing sound which indicated there was a thick growth of foliage hanging over the edge of the creek. It was almost pitch black and we had to do everything by feel. I took the rope in one hand and reached out toward the shore with my other one. My fingers closed around a small tree about the size of my arm. I tugged on it and it seemed to be stout enough to hold, so I looped the rope around it and put a good knot in it.

"Come on," I told Poudlum. "When we get off our boat we'll have to make our way through the woods until we get to their boats and the clearing."

We slipped into the dark and dense woods, feeling with our hands as we went. "Stay behind me and hold onto my belt, Poudlum."

It took a little time because we had to move extremely slowly, not only not to make any noise, but also to keep from falling or getting jabbed in the face by stiff, dead, or broken limbs lodged in the brush.

We emerged cautiously from the edge of the woods into the clearing, where we stopped and strained our ears for any sound of the men, but all we heard were the creek sounds—soft running water and an occasional frog croak.

Continuing to whisper, I told Poudlum I thought we could ease down the trail they had taken and see where it led.

"Hey!" Poudlum said, barely audible.

"What?"

"The moon ain't up yet, but I can see a little now. Why you think that is?"

I realized he was right and told him I figured our eyes were becoming more adjusted to the dark.

"You mean we getting to be like a cat that can see in the dark?"

"Something like that. Let's try moving along as quiet as a cat would, too."

Just before we entered the mouth of the trail leading

from the clearing, I thought of something. "Wait a minute, Poudlum. We need to do something first."

"Yeah, I 'spect we ought to do some praying."

"That too, but before we go let's take the paddles out of their boats so they can't chase us down the creek if we get caught."

"Now you talking! That's a mighty fine idea," Poudlum said.

There were four paddles in each boat. I told Poudlum we could hide them in the woods.

"Naw, that ain't good enough," he said. They'll have lanterns and might find 'em. Let's slide 'em into the creek and just let 'em float on down to the river, and maybe all the way down to Mobile."

We silently slid each long paddle into the water, giving each one a little shove when they began to float and watched them shoot out and disappear into the dark water of the creek.

When the last one was gone Poudlum snickered and said, "Now the Klan is truly up the creek without no paddle."

I grinned in the dark and said, "Come on, let's see what's up that trail."

We lifted our feet high with each step we took and put them down slow and straight to keep from tripping over any roots or rocks.

With our newfound night vision we could see the outline of the trail and the woods on each side of it. It wound on for what seemed like a quarter of a mile before we saw any sign of the Klan. But when we did, we froze in our tracks and gasped.

A great open field lay before us. There was a huge wooden cross burning in the center of it with what looked like several dozen or more hooded Klansmen surrounding it, each holding a burning torch.

"Lawd have mercy!" Poudlum exclaimed, a little above a whisper.

"Shhh!" I cautioned him. Then I leaned close and whispered in his ear, "No more talk, from here on out we communicate with signs, okay?"

He gave me a wide-eyed nod as I tugged on his sleeve and moved us into the edge of the woods. Once more we were making our way by feel, slowly and cautiously.

I had spotted the group of men we had followed up the creek off to the left, and we moved toward them under the cover of the dark forest.

Once again we were close enough to hear them speak, but they were strangely quiet as they stood in a huddled group.

I dropped to my knees and pulled Poudlum down with me. We sank down into the soft bed of the forest and peered out from underneath some low-growing bushes.

Poudlum poked me and motioned off to his left. I looked that way and here came the Night Hawk again. He still had his face covered when he walked to just within a few feet of our bulging eyeballs.

His knees were at eye level to us and I looked down and saw that beneath his robe he was wearing a pair of cowboy boots. The flickering light from his torch was reflecting off their silver-tipped toes.

I just about jumped out of my skin and I felt Poudlum

flinch next to me when the Night Hawk said, "I have been asked to intervene on your behalf before the Exalted Cyclops . . ."

His voice was deep and gravelly, like he had smoked too many cigarettes. He continued, ". . . who has informed me your petitions are being seriously considered and he has instructed me to present you before the Klavern for examination. Follow me."

The group marched off and Poudlum and I breathed sighs of relief. When they had moved off toward the center of the clearing we felt safe to whisper again.

"That Night Hawk still had his face covered," I said.

"Uh-huh, but I seen them boots he had on," Poudlum said. "From now on I be looking at everybody's feet."

"Yeah, me too."

Suddenly all torches were raised in unison and a mighty roar engulfed the clearing as the entire group gathered around the giant burning cross, and Poudlum and I just about had our breath taken away when we saw what happened next.

A hooded and robed figure, in brilliant red rather than white, appeared as if he had just walked from the flames of the cross itself.

"Look at that one!" Poudlum exclaimed. "How come he's dressed in red?"

"I think he must be the Exalted Cyclops."

"The what?"

"The leader, the one the Night Hawk said was considering the new men."

Sure enough, that's who he was and after a lot of ritual

stuff we couldn't hear very well, he announced the new men as citizens in the Invisible Empire and fellow Klansmen.

The ceremony was over and to culminate it, and to our shock and disbelief, the Exalted Cyclops removed his hood.

Unfortunately, the gasps we let out when we saw who it was were louder than we realized.

Chapter 4

The Chase

One thing we hadn't counted on was the Klexter. We found out later what he was called and that his job was to guard the outside perimeter of the Klavern.

It was our bad luck that in his circling he was right on top of us when we saw who the Exalted Cyclops was, and he had heard us gasp out loud.

Suddenly a loud voice not ten feet from our hiding place shouted, "Give the password and show yourselves!"

For a moment we were frozen to the ground with shock and fear. The entire horde of Klansmen turned in our direction as the Klexter pulled a pistol from inside his white robe and fired into the air.

The sharp crack of that pistol shot launched us into action. We leaped to our feet and went crashing back through the dark woods oblivious of anything that got in our way. We bounced off tree trunks, dived blindly through bushes, and clawed our way through clinging vines.

Our luck wasn't all bad. When we emerged onto the trail it was visible to us. The moon had come up and it lit our way as we ran like scared rabbits back toward the creek.

We skidded into the clearing, and past the three boats, but just before we hit the woods again Poudlum said between ragged breaths, "You think we ought to set them boats loose?"

I contemplated it for a moment, then we heard the beating of running feet on the trail behind us. "No time," I panted. "Let's get to our boat and get down the creek!"

The going was easier getting back through the strip of forest that separated our boat from theirs, and I breathed a sigh of relief when my hand closed around the rope I had moored the boat with.

"We gonna be all right, Poudlum. They can't chase us 'cause they don't have no paddles," I said as I began pulling the rope towards us.

That's when I became aware there was no resistance. Then the frazzled end of the rope where it had broken was in my hand.

Poudlum was real close to me and I held the end of the broken rope up close to his face so he could see what had happened.

"Told you that rope was rotten," he said. "We got to go get one of them Klan boats and paddle it with our hands!"

We turned to do that, but it was too late. Through the woods we could hear the voices and see the light of their torches and lanterns as they arrived at the creek.

We heard one of them call out, "They must have come in here by boat. Take one boat up the creek and two of them down the creek, 'cause I figure they must have followed us up here from the river."

Then we heard thumping sounds as they began to board their boats before one of them yelled, "Where's the paddles? Did one of y'all do something with the paddles?"

There was a moment of silence, then a voice said, "Looks like whoever it was took our paddles. You two, get on back up to the meeting and let 'em know what's happening and ask for help."

Poudlum said, "If we hadn't thought to dispose of them paddles we might be dead meat by now."

"We might still be," I whispered back.

"What you think we ought to do? We can't take off down the bank through the woods. They'll hear us for sure."

"Only one way to get out of here without making any noise," I told Poudlum.

"How's that? We gonna fly?"

"No, we're gonna swim."

"In the dark?!"

"We sure can't wait for daylight. What we can do is slip into the water real quiet like and just swim right on out of here."

"What about our shoes?"

"We'll take 'em off and tie the laces together around our necks."

"You think they gonna be any snakes in that water at night?"

"Naw," I lied. "They sleep at night. Let's get our shoes off and just slither on out of here like we're snakes ourselves."

It was with a small degree of dread that I slowly and quietly slipped into the dark water, and I could tell Poudlum felt the same way when he let out a small shiver as he joined me.

I was surprised the water actually felt good. I supposed it was because we were overheated with all the running we had done. As we treaded water I whispered as low as I could, "Try not to make any noise 'cause you know sound carries real good on the water, especially in the quiet of the night. We'll dog-paddle until we get well out of hearing. Let's stay close together and close to the bank. In case they figure out a way to get a boat after us we'll just get back on shore before they get to us."

As we dog-paddled along Poudlum said, "It's makes it harder to swim with all your clothes on."

"Yeah, it does," I whispered back. "Maybe we'll be able to pick up a log or something floating to hold on to as we go along."

In the moonlight, we could see the outlines of both banks of the creek.

Suddenly I saw the dim flash of light from something sticking out from the bank of the creek. It was the bleached wood of the blade of one of their paddles. I retrieved it and said, "Look at this, Poudlum."

I slid it across the water in front of us and we both rested our arms on it. "Now all we have to do is kick our feet and we won't get so tired."

After a while we were down the creek far enough that we didn't have to whisper anymore and were beginning to believe we were going to get away clean, but I still took the time to occasionally turn my head and look back up the creek. Once in a while we would stop dead in the water, and just listen for any sounds of the Klan chasing us.

One of those occasions Poudlum asked, "What we gonna do when we get back to the river?"

"I think we ought to stop at our campsite. We got dry clothes and something to eat there."

"I shore do wish you hadn't mentioned eating. I'm powerful hungry and all this swimming making it worse. I do hope some possum or some other kind of varmint hadn't got to our stuff."

"They can't eat the stuff in the cans," I told him.

"That's true, but they can make short work of our cheese and crackers."

Mainly just to get off the topic of food, I said, "You know what, Poudlum?"

"What?"

"I think we learned a valuable lesson tonight."

"Yeah," he said. "Not to go to no Klan meetings."

"I don't mean that. I was thinking about that rotten rope that caused us to lose the boat. The lesson is that it's a good idea to keep your equipment in good shape and pay attention to details."

"Yes," he agreed. "That's so. But speaking of details, do you think yo' Uncle Curvin gonna be upset with us for losing his boat?"

"Naw, he'll understand. Besides he wouldn't even have the boat if we hadn't told him where to find it after we helped Jake use it to get out of the county."

About this time I took another look back up the creek, and my heart soared when I saw what I saw. It was our boat. We had swum right by it. Anybody coming up the creek could have plainly seen it, but it wasn't visible to anyone coming down the creek because it had drifted up into a little cove across the creek from us.

When I pointed it out to Poudlum, he said, "Praise the Lawd!"

Now all we had to do was swim across the creek and get it.

We started that way and were slap dab in the middle of the creek, which was starting to get wide at this point, when we heard something that sounded like a giant horsefly coming down the creek.

We both knew what it was because we had heard the same sound on the creek where Poudlum had discovered the moonshine still.

It was a motorboat and it was coming fast, and we both knew we didn't have time to get to either bank before they got to where we were.

"Oh, Lawd," Poudlum exclaimed. "I do believe they got us!"

"Not if we go under," I told him.

"Not if we do what?"

"We got to go underwater. It's the only way," I said as I gave the paddle a shove toward our boat. "Dive deep and swim underwater toward our boat! Take a deep breath and do it now!"

I had swum under water before and had even opened my eyes while I was doing it, but never at night. It was the darkest dark I had ever seen, blacker than black, as I descended deep in the creek. I felt the vibration of the boat's motion and the motor as it swished by on the surface above me, after which I immediately began kicking and pulling for the surface.

When I emerged I saw the lights of the motorboat as it disappeared down the creek, then I turned round and round in the water, riding the wake of the boat, looking for Poudlum.

I was just about to panic when he finally burst up from the depths, spitting and spouting, closer to the boat than I was.

We both began swimming toward our boat and after we had grasped the side rail of it, Poudlum asked, "How we gonna get in it?"

"You go first," I told him. "I'll hold it to keep it from tipping, then after you get in you can pull me in."

After we got aboard we both just lay there in the dry bottom of our boat for a while, catching our breath.

Finally, Poudlum said, "Shore is glad to back on this boat."

"Yeah, me too."

I dimly saw Poudlum start moving about and he said, "This boat even got paddles."

"In fact, it has three now," I said as I reached over the side and snagged the one we had been floating down the creek on.

"You figure that motorboat be coming back this way any time soon?"

"Sooner or later it will," I told Poudlum. "But I figure they'll go up and down the river a while first. We ought to have time to get back to our original campsite. We'll cover the boat back up when we get there, get us some dry clothes on and break out them cheese and crackers."

"Sounds like a good plan to me," Poudlum said as we both grabbed a paddle.

We took the padding off the handles so we could go faster and began paddling hard. It only took us a few minutes to get back to our campsite, where we drug the boat up on the bank far enough so it couldn't drift off. Then we covered it back up with the saplings we had cut earlier.

All our gear lay undisturbed where we had left it. We were beginning to get chilled so the first thing we did was change into dry clothes. Then we broke the hunk of cheese in half and feasted on it with crackers in the moonlight.

"Shore would be nice to have a fire," Poudlum said after we finished our late dinner. "What time you think it is?"

"Probably about ten or eleven."

"Where you think that motorboat come from?"

"It probably come from further up the creek and belonged to some of the Klansmen who come to the meeting from up that way."

"Uh-huh, after one of the ones who didn't have no paddle run up that way and told 'em."

"Yeah, they probably thought we were in a paddle boat and they wouldn't have no trouble catching us."

"We would have been and they would have caught us if that old rotten rope hadn't broke."

I thought about what Poudlum had just said and realized he was exactly right. "You know what, Poudlum, you're right. We was real upset when we first realized the rope had broken and our boat was gone, but it turned out to be the best thing that could have happened to us."

"Uh-huh, looks like the Lawd was looking out for us. Hope he keeps on 'cause we ain't out of this mess yet."

No, we weren't, and we set to thinking and talking about what we should do next. What we finally decided was that we couldn't venture out on the river until that motorboat went back past us up the creek. And once that happened, we came up with a plan we would implement.

Since we were real tired, we decided to roll up in our blankets under the bushes and get a little sleep, knowing the sound of the motorboat would wake us up when it came back by.

I saw the moonbeams dancing off the water in the mouth of the Satilfa as my eyelids grew heavy. Poudlum was already snoring softly next to me.

In a deep and peaceful sleep I was dreaming I was at the old sawmill where I had first met mine and Poudlum's friend Jake, and I could hear the droning of the giant saw blade. Then the sound became more refined as I climbed toward wakefulness, and finally as I sat up fully awake, the sound turned into that of a motorboat speeding past our resting place.

"Wake up, Poudlum!" I said as I reached to shake his shoulder.

"Shoot, I'm wide awake," he said. "Who in the world could sleep through a racket like that? They must be going wide open."

"Yeah, it's late and I 'spect they wanting to get home," I said as I stood up and began to study the sky to see if I could figure out about what time it was.

The moon was glowing bright in a clear sky way up over

the river so I knew it was well after midnight, maybe one or two o'clock in the morning.

"That's about a brightest moon I ever seen," Poudlum observed. "Shoot, it's about light enough to pick cotton. We ought to be able to see good out on the river now. What time of night you think it is?"

When I told him he said, "You want to let's get on out of here while the gitting is good?"

"I think it might be a good time to do that instead of waiting for daylight. Let's get our stuff loaded on the boat."

The river was wide and bright as we paddled into it from the mouth of the creek. The current wasn't too strong, but it was still slower paddling upstream instead of down.

"Looks like it's pure silver in this moon light," Poudlum said between paddle strokes. "With nary a Klukluxter to pester us."

The river was quiet as a church when the collection plate is being passed. It was just Poudlum and me alone with the river, but some nagging little doubt kept popping up in the back of my mind, telling me that all wasn't right.

A few minutes later it came to me and I cried out, "Wait a minute!"

"Good Lawdy, what now?" Poudlum moaned.

"Those men whose paddles we took! They must have got some more paddles and I bet they put their boats in the water just like we did, which means they could be out here on the river right now!"

"Or, they could of paddled by while we was still sleeping," Poudlum suggested.

"That's true," I agreed as I looked back down the river

behind us. "On the other hand they could come up from behind us."

"They is a mighty big shadow that comes out a ways from the riverbank on the Choctaw County side, cast by the moon. If we paddled in that shadow couldn't nobody see us."

"That's a good idea, Poudlum. Let's get out of the middle of this bright river."

By and by we could see the dark outline of the road across the river from the ferry up ahead. At first I though it was lightning bugs, but as we stayed in the shadows and drew nearer we saw it was actually the light of several lanterns and some pickup trucks, and there was quite a commotion going on up there.

Chapter 5

Camp Visitors

We stayed in the shadow of the riverbank but got close enough to see what was going on. Sure enough it was the bunch of new Klan members whose paddles we had relieved them of. They were loading their boats onto the backs of their pickup trucks.

"So they did paddle by us while we was snoozing," Poudlum confirmed in a whisper. "Wonder where they got some new paddles."

"I 'spect some who come to the meeting from up the creek loaned 'em some."

Their voices had a tone of anger and frustration and we could hear an occasional cuss word.

Poudlum moved up next to me in the front of our boat and said, "Don't sound like they in too good a mood. I bet they expected to get home way before these wee hours."

I silently shared Poudlum's mirth as we watched their final preparations for departure from the river.

We waited until the last tail light had disappeared and the last sound had faded from up on the road before we paddled on up and beached our boat.

We flopped down on the cool grass and relaxed for the first time since we had heard the thumps of their paddles down at the mouth of the creek.

I was real sleepy and I knew Poudlum must be too, but I also knew we had some deciphering to do, so I sat up and said, "I don't think we ought to make camp here for the night, Poudlum."

"Ain't much of the night left," he said as he rubbed his eyes in the bright moonlight. "What? You think some of 'em might come sniffing around here in the morning?"

"That's exactly what I think, and we can't say we camped here all night because they came and went from right here."

"You think we ought to paddle 'cross the river and leave the boat next to the ferry? Won't nobody see us this time of night, and we could be at my house by daylight."

"No, that won't work. Too many people know we come down here. And besides, we done had our fishing trip ruined last year by them bank robbers, way up the creek. I don't think we ought to let the Klan ruin our fishing trip down here on the river."

That got Poudlum all riled up. "They done caused us to abandon a good camp and have a hunk of cheese for our supper instead of fried catfish. Caused us to have to swim down a dark creek and be up all night when we ought to be sleeping with a belly full of fresh fish."

He wound down, sighed deeply and said, "But I don't know what we can do about it except skedaddle out of here."

"We could go up the river," I said.

"Huh?"

"Yeah, we could go up the river a ways, find us a camp-site, build us a fire and fish all we want to, then if anybody comes around we'll just say we been there since we got to the river."

"Like we ain't never been down the river?"

"Nobody never seen us."

"I do believe that will work," Poudlum said as he stood up. "Glad we didn't unload the boat. Let's get on up the river and find us a good spot before it gets daylight."

We paddled about a half mile up the river and found us a spot on the Choctaw County side where a big cypress tree had been blown down into the edge of the river.

"Probably be some good fishing round that tree," Poud-lum said. "And look, ain't that a pretty good clearing right past the roots of the tree?"

I FIGURED IT WAS only about two hours left before daylight by the time we got a fire going and our camp secured.

I was wrapping myself up in my blanket next to the fire, so tired I ached, when the last thing I remember was hearing Poudlum say he was going to put out a line before he went to sleep.

I could tell it had been daylight for a while when I started waking up. The sun was already way out over the river, shooting little darts of sparkling light up from its surface.

After sight, the next one of my senses to come alive was smell. There was a delicious aroma in the air as I sat up. The source of it came from over towards our campfire where I spotted Poudlum frying fish in a skillet.

"Wake up, you old sleepy head," Poudlum said as he grinned and waved the skillet under my nose.

"Where did you get them fish, Poudlum?"

"I got 'em out of the river. You hungry?"

"So hungry I could eat a dead mule. How long you been up?"

"'Most an hour. Had two fish on the lines I set out last night. Come on and let's have us some breakfast."

While we munched on the delectable fish, Poudlum gave his account of our new campsite. "You know, this ain't a bad place to camp, and I reckon we ain't got much choice since the Klan done chased us out of our last one. I figure we can walk way out on the trunk of this big old tree, what done fell in the water, and tie us a trotline way out on it, and then run it across the water and tie it to that black gum tree up yonder," he pointed. "And we can troll up and down the bank in our boat, and I bet we catch us some fish."

"Them catalpa worms still alive?"

"Uh-huh. I stuffed some more leaves in the jars for them to munch on."

"What kind of leaves?"

"Just leaves off some bushes."

"You think they'll eat them instead of catalpa leaves?"

"Shore they will. They just fat worms and I don't think they can tell one leaf from another."

It occurred to me that Poudlum and I were making small talk, both of us reluctant to talk about what had happened to us last night.

We were licking our fingers when Poudlum said, "You remember everything about last night?"

It all flashed through my mind as I relived every vivid moment of it. "Yeah, I remember everything. Do you?"

"I 'member every bit of it. We thought we would get to see who a lot of 'em was, but we only got to see who the —what did they call him?"

"The Exalted Cyclops."

"Yeah, that's it! We gonna tell?"

"I don't know. If we need to we will. Let's just wait and see what happens."

"We know who one of the others was standing beside the Exalted Cyclops."

"Who?" I asked.

"Herman's daddy. Remember he told us his daddy belong to the Klan."

We put our camp in order, then we set and baited us a trotline like Poudlum had suggested. After that we fished from our boat up and down the riverbank until late in the day. We didn't have the same luck we had had down at the mouth of the Satilfa, but by the time the sun got low we had our bucket almost full of catfish.

Our catch was way more than we could eat, so we decided to paddle down and across the river and give them to Mr. Henry at the ferry.

He was piddling around tying up the ferry for the evening when we arrived.

"Looks like you young fellers had some luck," he said when we presented him with a big mess of fish. Dis gonna be more than enough to feed me and de missus and a few more. Mighty generous of you boys to think of me, and I appreciate it. Where y'all catch all dese fish?"

After we told him where our camp was, he asked, "So y'all ain't been down de river?"

Poudlum found a way to answer him without telling a lie. "We might fish some down that way before we get a bait of fishing, but right now we camped a little ways up on the other side of the river."

"Well, I'm proud to hear dat," Mr. Henry said. "De reason I ask is 'cause word in de Quarter early dis morning wuz dat some kind of a ruckus took place down de river and up de Satilfa last night."

He had my interest now. "What kind of a ruckus, Mr. Henry?"

"Some folks heard a gunshot going off and others say dey wuz a lot of coming and going on de creek."

I knew I shouldn't push my luck, but we needed to know, so I asked Mr. Henry, "You hear any more about it today?"

"Not about what de ruckus was about, but folks been mighty curious about who been crossing de river."

"What you mean?" I asked.

"Two mens I didn't know come down here 'bout mid-morning and wanted to know everything about everybody I took 'cross de river yesterday."

My heart skipped a beat when I heard him say that. "Did you tell 'em about us?"

"Naw. Dey asked me who crossed de river, not who paddled out on it."

I breathed a sigh of relief until I heard him say, "But I did have some mo visitors about noon, and dey was looking fo' you two boys."

When I heard what he said I desperately wanted to ask who it was, but I was struck dumb with fear.

Finally Poudlum stuttered it out for me. "Who-who-who they was, Mr. Henry?"

"It wuz dat boy 'bout y'all's age what lives up between Coffeeville and Center Point. Herman, Herman Finney, yeah, dat's his name. He said he wanted to fish wid y'all some, but he had his daddy wid him and he de one who ask most of de questions."

"What kind of questions?" I asked with dread.

"Just when y'all got here, what you had wid you, where you got de boat from, and had I seen y'all since. Sounded like he had some kind of special interest in you boys, so I thought you ought to know."

"We appreciate you letting us know, Mr. Henry. Has my Uncle Curvin come back from across the river yet?"

"Naw. He say it may be a couple of days fo' he gets back. It'll be tomorrow at the earliest."

"Would you please tell him we need to see him when he gets back?" I asked.

"Shore I will. I got a pretty good air horn on my ferry. How about I give it three long toots on my way 'cross de river to fetch him? You can hear it a good mile or more up and down de river. Dat way y'all could paddle on in and catch up wid him."

"That sounds like a good plan and we appreciate it, Mr. Henry," I told him as Poudlum and I prepared to launch our boat.

"Uh, one other thing," Mr. Henry said as we were pushing off. "If you boys need a place to come to, Poudlum knows where I stays down in de Quarter."

After we were well out on the river Poudlum said, "You think we might be in trouble?"

"I think Mr. Henry thinks we might be."

"Why you think that?"

"Because of everything he told us, and he same as invited us to hide out at his house if need be."

"You think some of them Klan folks gonna come looking for us?"

"Could be."

"What we gonna do?"

"We gonna stick with our story that we camped up the river last night, and we also gonna do what we come down to this river for. We gonna fish."

"That's what I say too," Poudlum said and promptly set about putting two trolling lines out as we paddled back towards our camp.

We had gathered us up enough fire wood to get us through the night and was just about to re-bait our trotline when we heard a motorboat coming up the river.

It got louder and pretty soon Herman Finney and his daddy beached their boat at our campsite.

"Uh oh," Poudlum said as his eyes grew large.

"It's all right," I told him. "Just let me do the talking," I added without hardly moving my lips.

Herman's daddy was a rough-looking man with a week's growth of dark whiskers. He wore a battered felt hat, brogans on his feet, and a pair of overalls with sawdust on them. I remembered hearing somewhere that he cut pulpwood for a living.

His eyes, partially shaded underneath the brim of his hat, surveyed our camp. Finally he said, "Howdy, boys."

My voice sounded more confident than I felt when I said, "Hey, Mr. Finney. Hey, Herman. Y'all out trying to catch a few fish before it gets dark?"

He squatted down with Herman standing behind him and began rolling himself a cigarette from a little sack of Bull Durham tobacco. When he finished, he put it in his mouth and lit it before he said, "I ain't fishing for fish, son. What I'm fishing for is information."

I didn't volunteer any for him, just waited to see what he had to say next.

"Is the fishing better up the river or down the river?" he asked.

"I can't rightly tell you that, Mr. Finney," I lied.

"So you and that boy over there," he nodded toward Poudlum. "Y'all been fishing up here since y'all got here yesterday?"

"There's the remains of our fire from last night," I said as I pointed to the mound of cold dark ashes.

"I noticed y'all got a piece of broken rope on the front of your boat. You lucky you didn't lose it."

"Yes, sir. We need us a new rope. Till we get us one we just drag the boat up on the bank so it won't get away."

He flipped his cigarette butt into the edge of the river and it made a little sizzling sound when the fire hit the water.

"So what you're telling me, son, is that y'all wasn't out paddling way down the river last night, down near where the Satilfa Creek empties into the river?"

I figured I had to tell another lie now, but I was saved

from doing it when Poudlum said, "I hear dey wuz some monster catfish down at the mouth of the Satilfa. We might fish down dat way tomorrow and see if we can catch a big one."

Mr. Finney stood up, pointed his finger at Poudlum and said, "Boy! Don't you know better than to speak to a white person without being spoken to?"

Poudlum turned silently away and walked over to the boats at the edge of the water while Herman's daddy continued to pepper me with questions.

After I told him we hadn't seen any other folks on the river, he gave me a stern warning that we better be careful because we were being watched.

I noticed that Poudlum was back beside me when they turned to leave.

When they got to the river's edge, Herman leaned over, looking into our boat, and suddenly said, "Hey, daddy! Come here and look at this!"

Chapter 6

The Broken Rope

What had caught Herman's attention was the three paddles in our boat. There was our two and the one we had captured in the creek and floated down it on.

Mr. Finney turned back toward us after he had observed this and said, "How come y'all got three paddles and one of them is white?"

"We found the white one floating in the water," I told him. Now that wasn't a lie.

"In that case I'll just relieve you of it since you don't need it," he said as he took the paddle and placed it into their boat.

My heart sank when he started his motor and pulled out into the river, because now he had a piece of evidence to connect us with being on the Satilfa last night. Some of those men might be able to recognize that paddle.

I told this to Poudlum as their engine noise faded away, and I was surprised when he said, "No need to worry about that."

"How come?"

64

"'Cause that paddle won't never reach the other side of the river."

"What in the world are you talking about, Poudlum?"

"Herman and his daddy will make it 'cause they can swim, but won't nothing else."

"Huh?"

"After he spoke like he did to me, and while he was still talking to you I drifted down to the side of the river."

"I remember that. What happened?"

"I noticed the plug in the boat was loose, so I just gave it a little kick and got it more loose. It'll probably pop out about halfway home and I didn't see nothing in their boat to bail with. It ain't too smart to go out on the river without a bucket to bail water with."

"I'm glad you sunk that boat, Poudlum, I don't blame you one bit. But I was wondering why you talked like you did in front of them, you know, kind of like you used to?"

"It ain't a good idea to act too uppity in front of white folks like Herman and his daddy. My new principal, Professor Jamison, said colored folks got to be able to speak two languages—depending on who's company we in, whether they be white or colored."

We found out later that Herman and his daddy both could in fact swim, and that incriminating paddle had floated off down the river while their boat, along with the motor, within sight of the ferry, had disappeared into the depths of the Tombigbee.

But in the midst of preparing our camp for the night, another horrible thought came to me. "Oh, no!" I cried out.

Poudlum leapt to my side and said, "What's the matter! You see a snake or something?"

"It's the rope. Remember Herman's daddy noticed our tethering rope was broken. The other end of it is still tied to that tree up the Satilfa. If somebody finds it they can match it up to the short end on our boat."

Poudlum promptly walked down to our boat and used his knife to cut the rotten rope loose, after which he returned and dropped it into our fire and said, "Can't match 'em up now."

"I wish I had thought to do that earlier, but he's already seen it, and if they find the end left on the tree, he can still match them up in his mind and know we really was down there last night."

"Is you saying we got to go back down there and get that broken rope off that tree?"

"As much as I hate to, I think we better," I told him. "We'll leave right after dark before the moon comes up. That way nobody can see us."

"How about coming back? The moon be up by then and it'll be light out on the river."

"Maybe it'll get cloudy. Let's get us something to eat. It ought to be good and dark by then."

We had our second meal of fried catfish after being on the river for nearly two days. We also had some baked sweet potatoes we had buried under the ashes of the fire.

When our bellies were full we decided it would be best to take all our gear and stores with us, even though we planned to return in several hours. Along with them we loaded a long slim piece of fat lighter to use as a torch to give us light to find the broken rope. Fat lighter was good for this because it consisted of the heart of a long-dead pine tree that contained a greater concentration of turpentine than the outer wood, which caused it to burn long and bright.

After we pushed off and began paddling downstream I told Poudlum I thought we ought to stay close to the riverbank until we got down to the mouth of the Satilfa.

"That's a good idea," he said. "That way we can see the gap in the trees where the creek comes in, then we can make a dash 'cross the river to it."

We reached the intersection of the river and the road, where we ceased paddling and listened for a few moments. Hearing nothing, we paddled briskly on downriver.

"Hope we don't hit nothing, paddling around out here in the dark," Poudlum said softly.

"Wouldn't be nothing but a log, probably, and this boat is pretty sturdy."

"Don't boats supposed to have a name?"

"I think they do. You want to let's give our boat one?"

"Yeah," Poudlum replied. "I think we ought to call it the Night Hawk."

"That sounds good to me, but I don't think we ought to paint it on the side anytime soon."

"Guess you right about that. But speaking of names, how you think this big old river got to be named the Tombigbee?"

"It's a Choctaw Indian word, or rather two of them."

"How you know?"

"My brother Fred told me."

"He tell you what them words mean?"

My brother had indeed told me what the name of the river translated into. Because of the nature of it, I didn't want to tell Poudlum while we were out on the river in the dark of night.

He sensed my hesitation and said, "Well, did he?"

I supposed I had to tell him because Poudlum and I would never dream of withholding any kind of information from each other. So I told him, "Yeah he told me. What it means in English is 'Coffin Maker.'"

Poudlum was silent for a few moments before he said, "Does you mean like a wooden box to bury dead folks in?"

"Yep."

"I sho' do wish you hadn't told me that. Wonder why anybody want to name a river something that spooky?"

"I'm afraid I don't know anymore about it than what I just told you."

"Now if we bump into a log I be thinking it's a coffin floating down the river with a dead Indian inside it."

Poudlum's dread was put to rest when we saw the dark outline of the gap in the forest directly across the river from us, signaling we had arrived at the spot where we needed to cross to the other side.

We paddled across the river without seeing or hearing anything, entered the mouth of the Satilfa, and were soon well up the creek.

"It's darker in here than it was out on the river," Poudlum said. "How we ever gonna find that little old piece of rope?"

"We'll recognize the clearing where they had their boats

beached and then we'll just backtrack from there."

We had no trouble recognizing that clearing because by the time we got there the moon had come up. While Poudlum lit the end of our makeshift torch, I guided us to the spot where we had tied our boat to the small tree with the rotten rope.

"Bring the torch on up here close, Poudlum, so I can see better."

I had my hand around the tree and it even felt familiar to me, but when Poudlum arrived with the torch, to my shock and dismay, the rope was gone!

"It's gone, Poudlum, somebody done beat us to it!"

"You sho' we got the right tree? It was mighty dark as I remember it."

"I'm certain. This is where we tied up and where we got in the water later."

In spite of my certainty, we searched up and down the bank until our torch grew short. Poudlum dropped the spent torch into the water and as it sizzled he said, "Guess ain't nothing to do but paddle on back to our camp."

"I reckon so," I told him and pretty soon we were gliding out of the mouth of the creek. Poudlum was talking to the fish as we left: "We'll be back, fishes. Y'all just stay put, 'specially you big'uns."

It was a long paddle back, going against the current, and as we neared our campsite we observed a strange thing from across the water. There was a big blazing fire which lit up the site and there were two men moving about where we had been camped. As we got closer I could see that one of the two was Herman's daddy, but the other one had his back turned towards us.

We ceased our paddling and remained undetected in the shadow of the bank.

"You think we ought to paddle on in some and see who the other one is?" I whispered. "Maybe see what they want?"

"'Bout like I think we ought to get drowned in this river!"

"What we gonna do then?"

"Paddle outta here real quiet like and go back down to the creek and make camp. It looks to me like they waiting for us to come back ashore at this camp."

I agreed with Poudlum and as we were gently turning the boat around I cast one last look back over my shoulder, and saw something that struck fear into my heart. The flames from the fire were causing little glimmers of light to reflect off the silver-toed cowboy boots of the one who was with Herman's daddy. It was the Night Hawk!

I was scared but I meant to see who he was. "Hold it, Poudlum! I want to get a little closer look before we go."

"Is you crazy?!"

"I believe that other one is the Night Hawk."

"What makes you think so?"

"Remember those silver-toed cowboy boots under his white robe up on the Satilfa last night?"

"Uh-huh. You certain that man's got on them boots?'

"Real certain. Paddle in real slow motion and we'll stay in the dark shadow of the bank until we can get close enough to see who he is. Try and be real quiet."

"I don't aim to even breathe," Poudlum whispered.

We inched closer and closer and finally we could hear their voices. Herman's daddy was saying, "You think they done skedaddled out of here? They didn't leave none of their stuff here."

"They might come back," the Night Hawk said. "We know they hadn't come back to Coffeeville, so they got to be out here on this river somewhere."

"Yeah," Herman's daddy said, "I hear they both do love to fish, so they could be out night fishing."

"We'll give 'em another half hour or so, then if they ain't back we'll cruise up and down this river all night if need be. They paddling and we got a motor on our boat, and we got spotlights. We'll find 'em."

No sooner had these words escaped the Night Hawk's lips than I felt Poudlum's hand on my shoulder. He leaned over and whispered into my ear, "Be right back."

Then to my astonishment he crawled over the side of the boat and disappeared into the dark water of the river!

I was beside myself for a few moments until I saw the dim outline of their boat rock a little in the water. I immediately glanced back at the two men to see if they had noticed. They hadn't, and continued talking when the Night Hawk said, "Who you reckon sent 'em out here?'

"They could have just been fishing and stumbled up on us," Herman's daddy suggested.

"Naw, I don't believe that's the case. Somebody sent 'em out here to spy on us, and I aim to find out who and why."

That's when I felt the boat rock and looked over and saw Poudlum's big eyes peeking over the side of the boat. I eased over to that side and gave him a hand climbing back into our boat.

Everything went well until he swung his second leg over the side and struck the glass jar full of catalpa worms, which made a clinking sound when it turned over and a rattling sound as it rolled across the bottom of the boat. The sound went flying across the water.

I snatched it up and stilled the racket, but it was too late. The two men jerked around, looking in our direction, and that's when Poudlum and I saw the Night Hawk's face in the bright light of the fire. Once again we both gasped in recognition.

"That's them!" Herman's daddy shouted. "They out there in the shadows. I'll get a spotlight out of the boat."

"Paddle hard, Poudlum," I whispered harshly. "It don't matter about the noise now!"

"No, just be real quiet and paddle easy," he whispered.

"But they gonna throw a light on us!"

"Uh-uh, they ain't gonna do that."

"Well how come not?"

"'Cause that spotlight be floating down the river."

"Well then they'll run us down with that motorboat!"

"Uh-uh, they ain't gonna do that neither, 'cause the gas line on the motor been cut clean in two."

When I realized what Poudlum had done, I reached over and gave him a pat on his wet shoulder, then we began paddling back down the river toward the mouth of the Satilfa. We heard their motor sputter once and then die.

We began making our paddle strokes long and deep when we got down the river a little ways. We figured they had paddles on their boat and even though their motor was disabled they could still chase us.

"Think they can fix that gas line, Poudlum?" I asked between paddle strokes.

"Naw. I didn't just cut it. I cut a chunk out of it and threw it in the river."

I breathed easier as we bent our backs and steered our vessel downstream. By the time we arrived at our original campsite inside the mouth of the creek we were worn down to a frazzle, what with all the paddling we had done.

"We could of done paddled all the way down to Mobile if we had been paddling in one direction," Poudlum said as we dragged our boat onto the shore.

After we got our blankets out of the boat we dined on little sausages from a can and soda crackers, because we were both ravenous. Afterwards we covered the boat up with the brush tops we had used before.

"Sure would be nice to have us a fire," I said. "But I suppose we better not take that chance."

"'Spect you right about that," Poudlum agreed. "But in the morning we can build us a small one as long as we use dry wood so it won't make much smoke."

I was already rolled up in my blanket when I heard Poudlum say, "I think I'll set out a couple of lines before I go to sleep."

In my state of exhaustion, just before I drifted off into a deep sleep, my last thought was that Poudlum was the only person I knew who loved to fish more than I did.

The next morning when I came awake I sat up with a start as the memories came flooding back, then I looked around and didn't see any sign of Poudlum anywhere.

"Poudlum," I called out real low.

"Over here," he answered as he emerged from past the boat holding a good three-pound catfish by the gills, its big head still glistening wet as it curled its tail upward.

"Looks like you done caught a big one!" I said.

"Got 'im on the line I set out last night. I'll dress him out if you'll start us a fire."

After we had devoured a big slab of delectable fish we set about pondering what our next move would be.

"I wish Uncle Curvin would get back. Maybe we'll hear Mr. Henry toot his horn sometime today. If so, we'll paddle directly up to the ferry."

"I got some bad news," Poudlum said as he was poking around in the boat.

"What?" I said in alarm.

"All the catalpa worms done died. On account of the Klan chasing us up and down the river our fish bait done died."

We whiled away the day and still caught a good many fish, even though we were using dead worms for bait.

About an hour before dark we still hadn't heard Mr. Henry's horn and were at a loss at what to do next.

Suddenly Poudlum said, "I know what we can do!"

Chapter 7

The Quarter

"What you got on your mind, Poudlum?" I asked

"We got enough time before dark to get through the woods up to the Quarter. I know where Mr. Henry stays. He'll know what we ought to do. We'll take him some catfish, too. Might even get us a good supper in trade."

After we had cut some green vines and plaited them together to make ourselves a rope, we looped it over a tree limb and suspended our food supply off the ground to keep it safe from varmints. We also drug our boat a little further into the woods and covered it up better before we set out.

We kept the riverbank in sight as much as we could as we headed through the woods. Sometimes we were forced away from it because of the denseness of the forest, but eventually the ferryboat side came into view.

We lingered in the edge of the woods until darkness came on, then we emerged and made our way up the road toward the Quarter, a place I had never been before, but knew about. It was where all the black folks lived, except the few who lived out in the country on farms like Poudlum's family.

The moon had come up illuminating the Quarter as we

entered it. We were on the narrow dirt road that was the main street. I noticed there were shallow ditches on each side of it, and I imagined how they would turn into muddy torrents when a hard rain fell.

The shotgun houses on each side of the road were weathered and drab without the benefit of paint, roofed with rusted sheets of tin. They were all built with small sagging porches in the front of three twelve-by-fourteen-foot rooms.

There were no glass windows, just wooden shutters hanging from the sides of the houses on rusted hinges.

I think Poudlum sensed my dismay as we walked down the middle of the little road. "This can be a mean place," he said. "But as long as you is with me everything be all right."

It dawned on me that the situation had reversed itself—instead of me protecting Poudlum in a white world, he was now protecting me in a black one.

A dim ray of light from a kerosene lamp seeped through the cracks of a closed window on one of the houses. Poudlum made a motion toward it and said, "Come on, this is where Mr. Henry stays."

"How can you tell? They all look alike."

"I been here a few times, bringing vegetables with my daddy. Got some kinfolks what stay in here, too."

We walked up the two rickety steps onto the porch and Poudlum tapped on the front door and called out, "Hey, Mr. Henry."

In a moment the door opened and there was the dim outline of Mr. Henry. "Hey, boys," he said. "I kind of thought y'all might drop by. Come on in de house. Y'all didn't run into nobody on the way, did you?"

"Naw, sir, nobody seen us," Poudlum replied as he held up our stringer with three big catfish on it.

"Lord, look at dem catfish!" Mr. Henry said. "Catfish two nights in a row! Let me take 'em back to de missus in de kitchen. She'll dress 'em out and fry 'em up for supper. You boys have a seat."

I looked around the room and saw a square table with the dim lamp on it. There were two wooden rocking chairs at the table and behind it a bookshelf with several worn volumes. There was also a wooden bench across the room up against the wall. Poudlum and I sat there until Mr. Henry came back.

He pulled his rocking chair over a little closer to us, sat down, rocked forward slightly and said, "You boys done stirred up a hornet's nest out on de river. Mr. Finney and dat boy of his come swimming up to de riverbank looking like two drowned rats. Said dey thought you boys had something to do with their boat and motor sinking. Once dat man quit spitting and sputtering, he did some masterful cussing. Y'all know anything about all dat?"

I glanced toward Poudlum and he gave me our secret signal that I should be the one to answer. "They did come by our camp, and Mr. Finney asked us some questions about where we had been on the river, but then they took off down the river so I don't know of anything I had to do with their boat and motor sinking."

Mr. Henry scratched his head and said, "What you boys think all this curiosity about y'all's coming and goings on de river is all about? Has it got anything to do wid dat ruckus down on de creek de other night?"

I gave our signal back to Poudlum and he proceeded to tell Mr. Henry about our experience on the Satilfa the night before. The only part he left out was the fact the Exalted Cyclops' identity had been made known to us.

"Lawd, save us!" Mr. Henry declared. "I think dat for some reason dey thinks y'all might have seen who some of 'em was. Anything else happen?"

I took over and told him how the two men had been at our camp last night after we returned from the creek where we had been searching for the piece of rotten rope. Once again, I left out the part about us also discovering the identity of the Night Hawk.

After that he told us if we had discovered who any of them were, he didn't want to know about it because the less he knew about the Klan the better. After he said that, I knew we had done the right thing, and I was apprecia-tive that we had an adult who would look out for us, but I still yearned for the safety of my uncle and the sanctuary of his truck.

"Why you think Uncle Curvin ain't come back yet, Mr. Henry?" I asked.

"Sometimes when he goes over to Choctaw County he comes back de next day, but sometimes he be gone as long as three or four days. I think you boys ought to spend de night wid me instead of going back out on de river tonight. And come tomorrow morning y'all probably ought to paddle on down de river to Jackson, and when Mr. Curvin gets back I'll tell him to pick y'all up at de bridge down dat way."

Poudlum looked at me before he said, "But Jackson is 'bout ten or fifteen miles on down the river."

"Dat's true," Mr. Henry said. "But paddling will be easy going downstream and it'll get y'all out of harm's way around here."

Poudlum looked at me again and I could tell he was thinking the same thing I was—that it would be a grand adventure to paddle down the river all the way to Jackson.

Mr. Henry got up, cracked the front door, and poked his head outside for a quick look-see. Apparently he was satisfied because when he closed the door he said, "Y'all come on and let's mosey on back to de kitchen. I 'spect de missus probably got some victuals ready for us."

We passed through the middle room of the house, which was the bedroom, and arrived in the kitchen where two lamps were burning brightly and the aroma of Mrs. Williams's cooking made my mouth water.

"Hey, Mrs. Williams," Poudlum said. "This here is my friend Mr. Ted."

She smiled brightly and said, "I know, I remember seeing him in church. Y'all sit yourselves down and I'll fix yo' plates."

I watched as she forked slabs of brown catfish fillets from a big black iron skillet on her wood stove. The grease was spitting and crackling as she spooned in the hushpuppies. "Won't take but just a minute for dem hushpuppies to cook," she said as she heaped piles of collard greens and black-eyed peas on our plates.

After we had feasted on all that wonderful food I noticed there was still a good stack of hushpuppies left over. While

Mrs. Williams was serving us a big slice of sweet potato pie she said, "I'll sack up de rest of dem hushpuppies and y'all can take 'em wid you."

Later on Mr. Henry escorted us back to the front room and gave us two quilts each, one for a pallet on the floor and the other for cover.

Before he blew out the lamp and left the room he said, "Folks will be wanting to cross de river right after daylight, so I'll get you young fellows up while it's still dark and once we get down to de ferry y'all can light out at the crack of dawn, get back to y'all's boat and be well down de river by de time anybody comes looking for de two of you."

I was dead tired and Poudlum must have been too because I heard his heavy breathing before I drifted off underneath the soft quilt.

At first I thought it was a storm with a lot of thunder, but when I became fully awake I realized the loud crashes were being caused by something on the tin roof of the house.

Poudlum was awake too. In the darkness I saw his form as he sat up and said. "That don't sound like no hailstorm to me."

Mr. Henry came rushing into the dark room whispering loudly, "You boys need to get up and get yo' shirt and pants on real quick. Make haste now!"

"What's going on, Mr. Henry?" I asked as I stuffed one leg into my pants.

"I 'spect it's de Klan. Sometimes late at night dey drive through de Quarter and chunk rocks on de roof of people's houses. But somebody could have seen you boys come here and dey could be looking for y'all."

He pressed a flashlight into my hand and said, "Use dis to find y'all's way back to your boat."

"But how we gonna get out of here?" Poudlum asked.

"Slide de wood box behind de stove over and y'all can slip through a hole under it and under de house, den sneak off in de dark. Dey may be watching de back door."

Just then there was a pounding on the front door and we could see the flickering light of a torch through the cracks.

"Now git!" Mr. Henry hissed.

Sure enough there was a square hole underneath the wood box. I saw Poudlum snatch the sack of hush puppies just before we slithered through the hole. When we were through we reached up and slid the wood box back over the hole.

When we peeked up from underneath the edge of the back porch, sure enough there were two pointy-headed robed devils standing there. We eased over to the other side and in the darkness made our getaway to underneath the back porch of the next house where we breathed a little easier because from there we could melt away into the darkness, but we froze when we heard a gruff voice coming from Mr. Henry's front porch say, "We heard the white boy and the colored boy what's been fishing down on the river stopped to pay you a visit tonight."

Mr. Henry was cool as a cucumber when he said, "Yes, suh, dem boys come by, brung us some catfish and we fed 'em a good meal. I 'spect dey back out on de river fishing by now. What you gentlemen be wantin' wid dem boys anyhow?"

"Never you mind about that, old man. If we find out you lying we'll stick this torch to this matchbox of a house."

"Oh, I'm telling de Lawd's truth. Dem boys is gone from here."

"We'll be watching you," the hooded Klansman said as he turned away. "Load up, boys," he called out. "Let's get out of this den of black heathens."

Poudlum and I watched as several hooded figures headed toward the pickup truck on the road.

"Like to take my knife to they tires," Poudlum whispered.

"Not now," I told him. "Just remember what the truck looks like."

From the light of their torches we saw the truck was a black Ford without a tailgate. While they were still milling around and loading up we lit out across the backyards of the Quarter.

Poudlum tripped over something in the dark and went sprawling, but as I helped him up I saw he had held on to the sack of hushpuppies. "You think anybody heard me?" he panted.

"Naw, I don't think so. I think we're out of their hearing by now."

That's when we saw the light and heard the engine of the truck on its way out of the Quarter. We lay flat on our bellies between two houses and watched them go by. It was an eerie sight seeing about six white-robed and hooded men standing on the back of the truck waving torches as they passed.

When the sound of the truck had faded away we walked

up to the road and very carefully made our own way out of the Quarter. When we got to Highway 84, the main road leading back to the river, we turned and headed that way.

"Don't turn that flashlight on yet," Poudlum warned. "We can see good enough to get to the river. Besides we need to save the batteries 'cause it's gonna be mighty dark going back to our camp through the woods."

We took turns walking backwards so we could detect anyone coming up on us in time to dash into the woods. When we got to the river we decided to sit down on the ferry and rest for a while before beginning our dark trek through the woods.

"Can you believe it?" Poudlum said. "The Klan has got themselves a spy in the Quarter! I bet Mr. Henry will flush 'im out."

"What you mean they got a spy in the Quarter?"

"How else the Klan know we at Mr. Henry's house? Some dirty rat seen us and went and told 'em, that's how."

We studied the position of the moon and concluded it was around midnight.

"On account of the Klan we can't get no rest and can't do much fishing. I purely do despise 'em, do you?"

"I reckon I do, Poudlum."

"I don't understand why grown mens be running around in the middle of the night clad in bed sheets and with a pillow case over their heads with two peep holes in it. What does the Klan want and where do they come from?"

"I know a little about where they came from," I told him.

"How you know?"

"Uncle Curvin told me."

"Naw! Don't be telling me Mr. Curvin is one of 'em!"

"No, no, Poudlum! I don't believe Uncle Curvin belongs to the Klan, but he does seem to know a lot about 'em."

"Then how come he knows—"

Poudlum was interrupted by the sudden glare of the headlights of a vehicle just before it crested the top of the hill behind us.

I sprang up and said, "We got to run for it!"

"It's too late!" Poudlum said. "We couldn't never make it to the woods before they gets here!"

Chapter 8

Burning Boats

I realized Poudlum was right. We could never make it to the woods before the lights would be squarely on us, so I called out in panic, "What we gonna do, Poudlum?"

"Gots to get wet," he said as he began sliding over the edge of the ferry which faced the river.

"Don't you get them hushpuppies wet," I told him as I followed behind him.

"And don't you let that flashlight get under water," Poudlum responded.

The river water was cool and I felt it soaking through my shoes as the vehicle's lights flooded over our heads and spilled out over the river. Then the engine ground to a halt and we heard two doors slam shut. It got awful quiet for a few moments, then there was a loud sound of wood scraping on metal.

"Sounds like they is unloading a boat," Poudlum whispered.

Sure enough that was what they were doing. We heard their grunts as they slapped it down on the muddy bank and then we heard the scraping again when it sounded like they were unloading a second boat.

Right after that we heard one of them say, "Well, we done our job. They'll be a buncha boys here early in the morning and they'll take one boat up the river and the other one down it."

"What they gonna do when they catch 'em?" the other one asked.

"They gonna make 'em tell who sent 'em to spy on us."

"What if they won't tell?"

"Oh, they'll tell all right once we get a holt of 'em."

The two men had walked out on the ferry and we could hear them very clearly, and their words scared me so badly I dropped the flashlight. When it hit the water it made a loud ker-plunk sound.

"You hear that?" one of them said.

"Yeah, I heard it. It came from off the front edge of the ferry. Let's take a look."

We could hear their steps on the wood of the ferry as they headed our way. It was one of those times when Poudlum and I didn't need spoken words to communicate. Just before the sound of their footsteps reached the edge of the ferry we both disappeared into the murky and dark water of the river.

I swam forward a little so I would be underneath the ferry and to my surprise I came up between two beams underneath it with enough space for my head to be out of the water. A split second later Poudlum's head popped next to me.

Once again we could hear their voices, but from above us now.

"I don't see nothing," one of them said.

"Yeah, must have been a big old fish or maybe a frog." the other one said. Then to our great relief the first one said, "Yeah, let's get on home. It's late."

After we heard the sound of their feet retreating from the ferry and the sound of the truck's doors slamming, we went back under water to get out from underneath the ferry, but didn't get out of the water until the sound of their vehicle had faded away in the distance.

As we sat in the moonlight on the ferry, soaking wet, Poudlum said, "We is in a mess now. Gonna have to walk through them dark woods with no light and wet as two drowned rats."

"We don't have to walk back," I told him.

"How come?"

"'Cause they is two boats right over there. We can just take our pick."

I could hear the mirth in Poudlum's voice when he said, "Or we can take 'em both, one for our flashlight and one for our hush puppies."

"You lose them hush puppies?" I asked.

"I turned 'em loose under the ferry. They wouldn't be no good soaked in river water. Let's get them boats in the water."

As we struggled to get the boats into the water Poudlum said, "You don't think this be like stealing, does you?"

"No," I told him. "I think it's more like survival. You heard what them two men said about us."

"About how they would make us tell who sent us? How we gonna tell something we don't even know?"

"Yeah, and they wouldn't believe us when we told 'em that. No telling what they would do to us."

"Well, this will make three boats they done lost to us. 'Spect they might run outta boats fo' long."

Once we had the two boats in the water we took a bailing bucket out of one and slung river water up on the bank to wash away our tracks, then we used the tethering rope and tied one behind the other. After that we climbed into the front one and started paddling.

We were shivering in our wet clothes once we got out on the river, but there was nothing we could do except paddle harder.

"I think it'll be all right to build us a fire," I told Poudlum. "It'll probably be around one or two o'clock in the morning by the time we get back to our camp."

"A fire would feel mighty good right now," Poudlum said.

"What we gonna do with these boats after we get there?" I asked.

I knew Poudlum was pondering on my question when he didn't answer for a while, so I just let him think. Finally he said, "We could burn 'em and have ourselves a real fire."

After we stopped laughing I suggested we could just turn them loose and let them float on down the Tombigbee.

"We could do that," Poudlum said. "But some of the Klan might live down the river and recover 'em."

"What if we just chopped a hole in 'em and let 'em sink?"

"I know how we could burn 'em and sink 'em both at the same time," Poudlum said.

"How in the world we gonna do that?"

"We could load 'em both up with a bunch of fat lighter, set it on fire, then turn 'em loose on the river. That way they would probably go on down the river a ways before they sunk."

I thought about his idea for a while and decided I liked it. "That sounds good, Poudlum, but we need to do it tonight. After we get a fire going we can make us a torch and pick up some lighter in the woods."

The mouth of the Satilfa finally loomed up ahead of us and we paddled thankfully into it and arrived at our campsite. Once we tied the boats up it didn't take us long to get a roaring fire going, then we retrieved our gear from where we had tied it to the tree limb and changed into dry clothes.

It took us a while to load the two boats with lighter, but once we did we tossed a burning torch into each of them. After the fires got to burning good we removed their tethering ropes and turned the two burning boats around so their bows were pointed toward the river and gave them a shove in that direction.

It was an eerie sight as we watched the current catch the boats as they slowly made their way out into the river.

We stood on the bank watching in awe as the flames leaped higher. They looked like two ghostly fireballs before they disappeared around the bend, where we knew they would soon sizzle and sink into the river, never to be seen again.

We settled down around our fire, grinning with satisfaction through our fatigue. After we had wrapped up in our blankets beside our fire I was almost asleep when I suddenly had an awful thought, sat up and said, "Poudlum, we got to move!"

Poudlum sat up, blurry-eyed, and said, "Got to move where?"

"Somewhere else. We got to move our campsite!"

"How come?"

"'Cause if they come up this creek and look real close they gonna see where we cut bushes down and used them to cover our boat."

"They ought to be just about out of boats. We done sunk three and one motor."

"They'll get more. They'll come with more boats with motors on them. We got to move!"

"Where we gonna move to?"

"I think we ought to move across the mouth of the creek and instead of cutting bushes to cover our boat, we ought to drag it up in the woods so our camp will be concealed completely."

"I thought we was gonna paddle down the river to Jackson."

"We will, but I think we ought to travel at night and sleep during the day tomorrow."

"That's a good idea. So far we been able to outthink 'em and outrun 'em, but they might be out here thick as moss on this river tomorrow. Let's get up and do it right now!"

The move was no fun because it was approaching the wee hours and we were tired from all the running and paddling we had done, but we made us another torch and loaded everything in the boat before we put our fire out.

Rather than attempting to hide the fact we had camped there, we just left the tracks of where we had dragged the boat down to the water.

Our thinking was that if we left an obvious campsite they wouldn't ever consider the fact that we were just across the water, but rather that we had lit out somewhere.

Poudlum held the torch while I paddled. When we got to the bank on the other side we saw that the underbrush was much thicker there, which was good.

We got out of the boat and transferred our stuff a little deeper into the woods than we had on the other side. We found a little clearing and hacked it clean with our ax, then we took our newly found ropes and used them to drag our boat through the thick foliage all the way to our camp, then we started ourselves a new fire.

It must have been three or four o'clock in the morning by the time we got ourselves settled and ready to finally get some sleep. But just before we rolled ourselves into our blankets Poudlum said, "I smell rain coming."

I had learned to pay heed to Poudlum's instincts so I said, "We better make us a tent with our tarp, then. We don't want to wake up wet."

As weary as we were, once again we put forth the effort to flip the boat upside down with all our gear and supplies underneath it. Then we cut a long straight sapling, trimmed it, and placed each end of it on the low limbs of two trees, after which we draped our canvas tarp over it and used pieces of our ropes from the Klan boats to secure the edges to stakes we had cut and driven into the ground.

"That's a mighty fine-looking tent," Poudlum said as he

stood back and observed it in the moonlight. "But we better gather some wood and put it inside. Be hard to start a fire in the morning with wet wood."

"It's already just about morning," I told him.

"Yeah, I can feel that in my bones," he said.

As exhausted as we were, we made that one last effort before we finally rolled up in our blankets again, this time under our tent.

"What time you think we ought to get up?" Poudlum asked.

"How about we just get up sometime after we wake up?" I answered.

"That sounds mighty fine to me," Poudlum said as he snuggled deeper into his blanket.

I did the same and it seemed like I was asleep before I even closed my eyes.

I had no idea what time it was when the pitter-patter of raindrops on our tent woke me up. I could tell it was daylight, but I had no idea how long it had been that way.

Poudlum was still sleeping when I crept outside to ponder our situation. It wasn't raining hard yet, but the fog was so thick it seemed like I could cut it with my knife.

I felt my way through the thick foliage down to the creek bank and almost fell into it because the fog was so dense you couldn't hardly see the edge of the water. I went back and dug our food sack out from underneath our boat and when I got back to the tent Poudlum was sitting up and rubbing his eyes.

"What time of day you think it is?" he asked.

"I ain't sure, probably late morning and way past

breakfast time," I told him as I began digging around in the sack.

It wasn't cold, but there was a slight chill in the air, so we started a small fire before we breakfasted on canned sardines, canned beans, and saltine crackers.

"These little salty fishes is tasty," Poudlum said. "But they ain't catfish. I think I'll catch us some after we finish eating."

"What you gonna use for bait?"

"I'll find a rotten tree and dig out some grub worms."

"It's so foggy you can't half see, so I guess it'll be all right 'cause won't nobody be out in this weather."

"Good," Poudlum said as he wiped his mouth. "I'll go set out a line or two."

"How you gonna catch a fish with it raining?" I asked.

"It ain't raining underwater. The fish don't know it's raining," he said as he headed toward the woods to look for bait.

I went in the opposite direction to gather more firewood before it got real wet. By the time I got back to the tent with an armload of lighter knots Poudlum was back from the creekbank.

"What did it look like out there?" I asked.

"It look like Mother Nature giving us a break. That fog done covered us up with a blanket so thick can't nobody find us. But I was also thinking they might be thinking that we thinking won't nobody come looking fo' us in this weather, so they might come anyway, 'cause of what we thinking."

It took me a few moments to unravel what Poudlum

had said, but then I said, "We done prepared for that situation."

"Huh? How we done that?"

"By moving over here to our new camp. Even if they are looking for us all they'll find is the deserted camp across the mouth of the creek. If they find it they'll think we left and they won't know whether we went up the river or down it."

The rain got serious about that time and began to pepper our tent hard and steady. We were isolated from any wind because the surrounding forest protected us, and we had placed the tent on a small knoll so rainwater would flow away from us.

I tossed a lighter knot on the fire and sparks flew up for a little while before it exploded into flames.

"I like them lighter knots 'cause they hard as a rock and burn for a long time. What you reckon makes 'em burn like that?" Poudlum asked.

"They got turpentine in them," I told him.

"Who told you that?"

"My brother, Fred."

"Well then, I 'spect it be true if Fred said that."

"He said the turpentine concentrates in the pine tree's stump, its heart and the knots, which is the bent elbow part where the limbs are attached to the trunk. He even said it could be ground up and used in dynamite."

"I wish we knowed how to do that, then we could light 'em and toss 'em into some Klan boats."

Poudlum caught a monster catfish later on and the two fillets dressed out to about a pound each. We didn't have any fear about the smoke from our fire because of the rain and the fog.

After we had eaten our fried catfish dinner Poudlum said it was the second best thing he had ever put in his mouth. When I asked what was the first he said it was the catfish we ate last night.

Later on it got to be kind of boring just sitting in the tent and listening to the hard rain pounding on it.

"We needs something to do," Poudlum said.

"What you got in mind?" I asked.

When he said it, as on some other occasions, I couldn't believe what came out of Poudlum's mouth.

Chapter 9

The Storm

"I wants you to tell me everything you knows about the Klan," Poudlum said.

At first I was astounded by what he asked me, but then I considered his point of view, his wondering at the causes which made grown men chase boys up and down the river, so I resolved to do the best I could with my limited knowledge, but I still wasn't in any hurry to get started.

"I don't know a lot, Poudlum, and I ain't sure what I do know is what really happened, but what I do know come from my brother Fred and my Uncle Curvin."

"I 'spect it would be mostly right then," Poudlum said.

It was mighty cozy in our tent, being high and dry with a small fire, while the rain continued to pour from an overcast sky.

"I like it in our tent," Poudlum said. "It kind of makes you feel safe and secure like it did when we used to get in the hidey-hole way up the Satilfa under the Iron Bridge."

"Yeah, I know what you mean. I'm sho' glad Uncle Curvin thought to put this tarp in the boat."

"You think he ever gonna get back from over in Choctaw County?"

"Not today he won't. They won't be nobody crossing the river in this weather. I figure wherever he is, he'll stay there until it clears up."

"I thought we was gonna talk about the Klan?"

"What you want to know?"

"Nothing in particular, just start way back as far as you knows."

"From what I've been told it was started back during Reconstruction in the South after the Civil War ended."

"Seems funny they calls it the Civil War. From what I learned in school it was most uncivil."

"You got me there, Poudlum. Uncle Curvin don't call it that, he calls it the War of Northern Aggression."

"Don't matter what it was called. Let's get back to the Klan."

"Okay, what I heard was that after the war it was a time of corruption and destruction of society, a time when folks had no protection by the law for their property or even their lives, and the Klan was organized to keep all that from happening."

"How come all that was happening, if it was?"

"Because of the vengeful laws passed by the Congress, which made it unlawful for Southern white men to hold public office. Because of them laws all the public offices was filled by carpetbaggers from up north."

"What you been taught a carpetbagger is supposed to be?"

"I think that was what people from up north, the ones

who came south just to make a big profit, was called."

"So you saying the Klan came into being to protect decent folks after the war was over?"

"That's what they say."

"That ain't how Professor Jamison tells it. He says that after the Civil War some white folks in the South used the Klan to get power back in politics and keep control over the freed slaves. He says they threatened, beat, and even killed folks till they got what they wanted."

"Uncle Curvin said ain't no need for the Klan nowadays."

"Then how come they come down in the Quarter and pester folks like they did last night?"

"Nobody never give me the answer to that, Poudlum. But I 'spect it may just be bred into 'em or they just stuck in the past. It could also be they are afraid of change that's coming, but to tell you the truth, I really don't know."

"One thing we does know," Poudlum said. "We knows they is chasing us 'cause they think we discovered who the Exalted Cyclops is. What they don't know is we know who the Night Hawk is, too."

"You hit the nail on the head. They also think we was spying on 'em on behalf of somebody else, and ain't nothing we can say or do gonna change their minds on that."

"So what we gonna do?" Poudlum asked.

"We got to come up with a plan and stick to it."

We spent the remainder of the dreary day considering and reconsidering our options. What we finally decided was we would paddle on down to Jackson, but would take our time about it and travel at night as long as the weather permitted. Along the way we would seek out another good campsite where we could be concealed, and get in as much fishing as possible.

Once we hooked up with Uncle Curvin we would get him to take us to see our lawyer.

Poudlum and I did have a lawyer. He was Mr. Alfred Jackson, who had represented us and sprung us from Sheriff Elroy Crowe's jail, and he had also invested our reward money for finding the money Jesse and Frank, the bank robbers, had hidden in the Cypress hole way up the Satilfa Creek from where we were now. He let it out for interest so me and Poudlum, along with my brother, would have money to go to college on.

Actually it had been Uncle Curvin who had found the money, but he couldn't have done it without our help, and he had given us credit for it.

Mr. Jackson had told us to come see him if we had any troubles, that his door would always be open to us. He was an elderly lawyer who provided a lot of free legal service to poor folks, white and colored alike, so we admired him very much.

"Mr. Jackson will know what we ought to do," Poudlum said. "What time of day you think it's getting to be?"

"I don't rightly know," I told him. "Hard to tell without being able to see the sun, but I think it's getting on close to dark. What you think?"

"My belly is telling me it's about suppertime."

We inventoried our food supply and found we had a big hunk of cheese left, several slim boxes of crackers, four flat cans of sardines, three cans of beans, and a half-dozen cans of sausage. That's what we dined on that night, the sausage with crackers and cheese, while the rain continued to pour down in torrents.

We retreated to the center of our tent to escape the dampness and threw a couple of lighter knots on the fire. Just before we drifted off to sleep Poudlum said, "This rain keep up like this, the river gonna be swelled up like a dead possum."

It continued to rain hard all night and when morning came it was still overcast and drizzling.

Poudlum got our breakfast off one of the lines he had set out while I stoked up our fire.

While we were munching on the sweet fish fillets Poudlum said, "Look like this weather done set in. If the sun don't come out soon we gonna get all mildewed and moldy."

We smoothed off a place on the ground and played mumblety-peg until we tired of it. After that we sat around and told a few stories until we became weary of that, too.

About when we thought it ought to be noon, the rain stopped and a sliver of sunlight peeked through the dark clouds.

"Look at that," Poudlum said as we peered out the end of the tent at the sun rays filtering through the trees. "Now that's more like it. It ought to clear up good by nighttime and we can head on down the river."

Within an hour there was bright sun flooding down on us from a clear blue sky. We flipped the boat right side up and hung our damp stuff on tree branches to dry. After it dried we packed it all up inside the boat and were prepared to light out down the river as soon as the moon came up.

We also cut the long, slim lighter-hearts out of some dead pine trees and loaded us up a half-dozen six-foot-long poles to use as torches if we needed them. We were all ready to depart, but the trouble was, we had several hours before we could.

After we folded up our tarp we placed it next to the trunk of a big tree and sat down on it so we wouldn't get the seats of our pants wet.

As we were sitting there leaning back against the tree trunk Poudlum said, "I purely do despise to have to sit here with nothing to do—nothing to occupy our minds."

"Why don't we just sit and talk about whatever crosses our mind?" I asked

"That's fine by me. What you want to talk about?" Poudlum responded.

"I don't know. Oh, yeah, I read where you got a new principal at your school, that he had been one of them colored pilots in the war, the ones that went to school up at Tuskegee."

"Uh, huh, that would be Professor Jamison," Poudlum said with a good amount of pride in his tone of voice.

"Does he ever talk about the war?"

"He does sometimes, but nothing about shooting and fighting."

"Well, what does he talk about then?"

"He talks a lot about what it was like over in Europe and up north, about how it was different from down here in the South."

"How did he say it was different?"

"For one thing, me and you would be going to school

together, and they don't treat colored folks like they all one big ignorant lot."

"What else does he teach y'all?"

"That things are gonna change 'round here and we got to do a lot of hard work to get ready for it and make the best of it."

"Colored folks already do a lot of hard work."

"Uh-huh, they do, but the professor is teaching us to work hard with our minds, and to act proper as well as speak proper." Our talk kept us occupied until we saw the moon come slipping up over the treetops. We got up and walked to the boat, which was closer to the water, then we stopped dead in our tracks when we heard the sound. It was a swishing and hissing noise, approaching a small roaring sound.

Poudlum said, "What you think that noise is?"

"I think it's the sound of the creek," I told him.

"The creek is rising from all that rain!"

We slipped through the bushes and found the creek had risen several feet and was a raging torrent before us.

"What you think?" I asked Poudlum as we gazed at it.

"Might be all right after we get out on the river, but the creek is flowing mighty swiftly."

Neither of us wanted to spend another night where we were because if we did we would have to stay put all day tomorrow before we could start traveling on down to Jackson tomorrow night. We were anxious to get on down that way and hook up with my uncle and get away from the Klan, so we agreed to give it a try.

After we had dragged the boat to the water's edge

Poudlum said, "We got to be real careful 'cause that water is moving faster than a cat with his tail on fire!"

We eased the nose of the boat into the water and could feel the tug of the rushing water, then we got behind it, planted our feet on the solid ground, gave a mighty shove, and leapt aboard.

The powerful surge of the water caught us immediately and turned the boat sideways and water was lapping up over the right side and into the boat. We grabbed our paddles and righted the boat a moment before it capsized.

"Hold her straight!" I yelled at Poudlum as we fought the water with our paddles.

The swiftness of the current shocked me, but I thought it would ease when we exited the mouth of the creek out into the river.

I was wrong. As the creek swept us out into the river the raging water increased in its intensity and our boat was swept downstream as if it were some kind of toy. The current of the swollen river compared to the creek was like comparing a mouse to an elephant.

"I think we done made a mistake, Poudlum!" I yelled out.

"Uh-huh, a big one," he yelled back. "What we gonna do?"

"Ain't nothing we can do except try to use our paddles to keep pointed downstream."

"Rate we traveling we'll be in the Gulf of Mexico before morning," Poudlum yelled as we fought the current.

We barely kept from capsizing several times and it was all we could do to keep our boat pointed downstream.

There was a bridge over the Tombigbee in Jackson, the place where Mr. Henry had told us he would tell Uncle Curvin to meet us. Sometime before daylight the mighty current of the river swept us underneath it and into a part of the river where we had never been.

Not long after that our arms gave out and we had to just let the current take us. By then the moon had set and we were engulfed in total darkness, and we moved to the middle of the boat and huddled close together as we awaited whatever fate had to offer us.

We expected to be capsized and have to swim for it, or to be rammed and sunk by some gigantic log, but to our surprise we came to a soft landing. It felt spongy when we hit it and we were engulfed in something which felt leafy and giving.

We could still hear the sound of the current rushing by, but it did seem to have abated somewhat. In the meantime we had come to a complete halt and were very fearful of where we were. Poudlum dug out a box of our wooden matches and lit the end of one of our torches. When the flame caught and burned bright enough to see, we discovered we were lodged in the upper branches of a giant oak tree which had collapsed into the raging river.

"As long as it don't tear loose from the ground completely it ought to hold us," Poudlum said.

"You think we ought to tie up to one of these big limbs?" I asked.

"Uh-huh," he answered. "But we'll put a little slack in the rope so if the river goes down we won't be hanging from a tree."

We tied the boat up real secure to one of the giant limbs and by the light of our torch we ate a can of sardines and some soggy crackers.

The current was still raging, but once again we had found a little sanctuary, kind of like the hidey-hole underneath the Iron Bridge. After we finished eating we dug out our blankets and rolled up in them in the bottom of the boat.

"I ain't never been this tired before," Poudlum mumbled as in our exhaustion we drifted off to sleep.

"Me neither," I told him. "You remember us going past the bridge in Jackson?"

"I do. Maybe tomorrow morning, if this river quiets down some, we can paddle back up that way and wait on Mr. Curvin."

"You think the river will be down by morning?"

"Maybe. It'll probably quiet down just as sudden as it rose up."

"My arms feel like they too tired to ever do anything again. How about you, Poudlum?"

"Yeah, mine too. Fighting that river was worse than picking cotton."

The river did sound like it was slowing down and I told Poudlum I expected everything would be back to normal in the morning.

He agreed with me just before we drifted off to sleep.

But we were both wrong.

Chapter 10

Silas and Dudley

No matter what kind of turmoil is going on around a human being, they eventually reach a point of exhaustion whereby they collapse into a deep sleep. That's what happened to Poudlum and me on the rushing river while we were hung up in a downed tree a couple of hours before dawn.

The dim light of a foggy dawn was upon us when I felt movement. At first I thought we had broken loose and were floating further on down the river. But then the sound of our boat crunching onto solid ground brought me to full awareness.

I bolted up from the bottom of the boat the same time as Poudlum, and what we saw just about scared us half to death.

There was a dim figure on the bank of the river, who had pulled us up on the shore using our tethering rope, and he was tying the rope to one of the protruding roots of the fallen tree we had crashed into.

He raised up and said in a gravelly voice, "Looks like you boys got caught in that there storm. Y'all are mighty

fortunate to have got tangled up and caught up in this big
old tree."

I rubbed my tired eyes, got them focused and saw a face
which I couldn't tell if it was a dingy and dirty white one
or a colored one, but from the way he talked I suspected
he was white.

"You boys come on up to the house and get yourself dried
out," he said. "My name is Silas. Who might y'all be?"

I struggled to shake the grogginess from my mind before I said, "I'm Ted and this is Poudlum. We were fishing
up the river and the current caught us up and landed us
in this tree."

"That's what I figured," Silas said. "Why don't y'all grab
all your stuff and follow me?"

We did like he said and after a short walk we came upon
a shanty with a saggy porch and a leaning rock chimney
on the side of it. When he saw us hesitating he said, "I got
a fire going and it's good and dry inside."

He climbed the rickety steps to the porch and opened a
door constructed of three wide boards going up and down
and held together by two short boards nailed across them,
one at the top and one at the bottom.

"Make haste, boys," Silas said as he held the door open.
"It's damp and chilly out here."

We reluctantly followed him inside and he closed the
door behind us and dropped the wooden latch with a soft
thud.

There was a kerosene lamp burning on a bare table in
the middle of the room, which gave off a little more light
than the foggy early morning had outside, and I could see

that Silas had on a pair of faded and dingy overalls with one gallus hooked over his shoulder and the other one hanging loose, with no shirt on underneath. That's when I saw for sure he was a white man as the lamplight reflected off his pale white shoulders.

Across the room there was a good fire going in a sooty limestone fireplace, and in spite of the shabbiness and stale smell of the room, it was warm and inviting.

"You boys been on the river all night?" Silas asked as he removed his shapeless and sweat-stained felt hat, which revealed long but thin and stringy hair hanging down to his neck.

His short beard was patchy surrounding his thin-lipped face, framed by bushy eyebrows and a big flat nose, which looked like it had been smashed in a few times.

"Y'all just put your stuff on the table," he said. "Take your blankets and just curl up on the floor next to the fire and get yourselves some shuteye. I figure y'all have to be plum tuckered out. The river ought to be going down enough by late today so y'all can paddle back up to where you come from. By the way, where did y'all come from?"

"Up at Coffeeville," I said without thinking.

While Silas was adding some logs to the fire Poudlum leaned close and whispered, "Shouldn't have told him that."

"I know," I whispered back.

"I don't think I like Silas or this place," Poudlum whispered again.

"Might not hurt to just rest a while," I told him.

Suddenly Silas raised up from the fire and said, "What y'all whispering about?"

"Nothing," I responded. "Just talking about how lucky we are you stumbled upon us."

"You right about that, son. How long y'all been asleep in that boat before I come upon y'all?"

"Two or three hours I reckon," I told him.

"Guess y'all mighty tuckered out. Well, go on and lay yourselves down and I'll wake y'all up by noon and we'll have us a bite to eat. Then we'll see what the river looks like and if it's calmed down enough for y'all to paddle on back toward Coffeeville. That's a mighty far piece and take y'all two or three days paddling hard."

I didn't feel real good about it, and I could tell Poudlum didn't either by the way he was casting his eyes around the shadowy room. But our fatigue got the best of us and we stretched our blankets out on the floor and rolled up inside them.

The sound and warmth of the fire was like food and drink to a starving person and it immediately took its toll on me. I looked across and saw Poudlum's eyes were flickering in unison with the flames in the fireplace.

In that paralyzing state between wakefulness and sleep I let my eyes give the room one last survey. Silas was rummaging around at something on his cot against the far wall. That's when I noticed there was another cot beyond his and it looked like there was a big lump on it, and just before I succumbed to slumber, I thought I saw the lump move.

The fire had died down when I woke up and I could see that sometime during our long nap Poudlum and me had cast our blankets aside. As I raised up on one elbow I heard something bumping and clanking behind me. Poudlum was still asleep when I rolled over to what was making the racket.

Once I did I immediately wished I hadn't, because the sight that met my eyes was enough to scare a body clean out of his wits. Little goosebumps popped up all over me and I could feel the fine hairs on the back of my neck standing erect.

The bump I had seen on the cot past the one Silas used early this morning was alive and he was emptying our sack of food-stores out onto the little table, making a heap of noise as he sorted the beans, sardines, and little cans of sausage.

But it wasn't his taking possession of our food supply that scared me, it was the shape of him. He was a short man with little short legs and little short hairy arms, and he was also very fat and the perfect shape of a goblin if I had had to dream one up.

His matted hair splayed out in all directions reminding me of a big black grease spot on a wooden kitchen floor. He must have sensed I was watching him, for suddenly he stopped all movement, then jerked around to face me.

I just about jumped out of my skin when he did that and I saw his big bug eyes, which reminded me of a giant frog, and on top of that they were crossed and I couldn't tell if he was really looking at me or off toward the other side of the room.

His belly stood out like a pot leg on a wood stove and above it decayed and snaggled teeth protruded from his open mouth, and I thought to myself this was just about the most unattractive human being I had ever beheld.

About that time I heard Poudlum rousing up behind me. When he sat up and observed the goblin, in his state of fear he said, "It appears the Good Lawd has done forsaken us and let us float down the river to hell!"

The goblin didn't seem to hear him and spoke for the first time. "I see y'all done woke up."

It shocked me that he could actually utter words and it took me a moment before I could muster up the courage to respond, but I finally stuttered, "We-we-we have. Uh, where is Silas?"

"He be out taking care of bidness," the goblin replied.

"What kind of business?" I asked.

"The kind of bidness that ain't no bidness of yourn," he responded.

Poudlum finally got the courage to speak and said, "Well, who in the world are you?"

"I be Dudley, Silas's brother. He takes care of me."

That's when I realized Dudley did not have all of his faculties and was actually a child in his mind while in years he appeared to be middle-aged.

That's when Poudlum poked me and whispered, "We need to get on out of here."

We stood up and I told Dudley, "We appreciate y'all's hospitality, and now we need to be getting on back up the river."

"Uh-uh," Dudley grunted.

"Huh?" I asked. "What's that you said?"

"Silas say for y'all to wait till he comes back."

"But we got a long way to go and we need to get to our boat," I told him.

"Silas be gone in y'all's boat."

"He took our boat?!" Poudlum exclaimed.

"Uh-huh. His boat got sunk in that storm what just ended."

"Dudley," I said. "Where do you think Silas went in our boat?"

"Told you, he taking care of his bidness."

With that said, Dudley whipped out a knife with a big shiny blade from his boot, and Poudlum and I shrank back in fear. But he simply took it and stabbed it into a can of our beans and carved the lid off. Then he licked the blade and turned it on a can of sardines as he said, "I'm fixing to partake of some of this grub y'all brought. You boys want to join me?"

I was starving and I figured Poudlum was too, but I knew I had rather eat dirt than dine with Dudley. Poudlum confirmed my suspicion when he made a gagging sound from behind me.

"Uh, you go ahead, Dudley. We had something earlier on the boat," I lied.

It wasn't a pleasant sight watching Dudley gobble up our food. After he finished and let out a huge belch, I asked him, "Say, Dudley, do you think it would be all right if we step out on the porch and see what the weather is like?"

"Naw," he said. "Silas say for me to keep y'all inside."

"I believe we're being held captive!" Poudlum whispered.

"You think we ought to make a dash for the door?"

"I 'spect not 'cause he might whip out that big blade if we did," Poudlum said.

While Dudley was carving open a can of sausage I whispered to Poudlum, "Let's just play along and something will open up for us."

In a little while after Dudley had stuffed himself on our food we noticed he was nodding off while seated at the table.

I signaled to Poudlum and he began to creep along the wall to the right and I did the same to the left. Our plan was to circle around Dudley and dart out the front door.

We were almost there when he leapt up and darted over to block the front door quicker than a water bug.

He stood there, back to the door, knife in hand and said, "I done told y'all Silas said not to let you out the front door."

We both froze and I knew we had to think fast if we wanted to outwit a halfwit. My eyes searched the room and lighted on a door at the back of the room. I figured it must be the back door leading out of the shack.

"How about that back door, Dudley?" I said. "Silas didn't say we couldn't go out it, did he?"

A bewildered look came over his face for a moment, then he said, "Naw, he never said that."

"Then how about we go out that door over there," I said, pointing.

"I reckon it'll be all right," Dudley said with a befuddled look on his poor face. "He didn't say nothing about y'all not doing that."

"Then we just gonna walk over there and ease out that

door and you can have all that food we brought, okay, Dudley?"

"I reckon that'll be all right," he told me with a blank look.

"Ain't no need for that knife, Dudley," I told him. "Just put it away and save it to open all those cans of food we brought you."

We were highly relieved when he slid the blade back into his boot and said, "Y'all really gonna leave all this food here?"

"That's right, Dudley. You can have it all for yourself. We'll just go out that back door and be on our way. And tell Silas he can have our boat to take care of his business in."

While I was talking Poudlum and I were slowly edging along the wall towards what we thought was the back door.

"How y'all gonna get back up the river without your boat?" Dudley asked.

"We'll walk through the woods over to Highway 84 and then just follow it to the ferry landing in Coffeeville"

I was just making something up to pacify Dudley, but when I heard what I had said it did sound like it could be a plan.

We were getting real close to that back door. A few more steps and I had my hand on the latch.

"You ready?" I mouthed to Poudlum.

When he nodded I lifted the latch and flung the door open.

What shocked me was just before we darted through it, Dudley came speeding across the room, like the darting of a snake's head just before the bite, hit us both in the back and drove us through what turned out to be the door to a back room instead of to the outside.

We crashed to the wooden floor and got splinters in our hands when we used them to break our fall.

Before we could look around the door slammed shut and we heard the latch fall into place.

I had to agree with Poudlum when he said, "I do believe we done been outwitted by a halfwit."

Chapter 11

Trapped

It was pitch black in that room. As I felt around with my hands I could feel the floor was put together tightly with thick pine boards, and there was no light seeping in from any other door or window.

When I recovered from the shock, I told Poudlum that I wished we had some kind of light.

"I got some wooden matches in my pocket," he said. "I'll strike one soon as I pick these splinters out of my hands."

In a moment, I heard him scrape the head of his match across the floor, and it flamed to life and illuminated our prison. I had been right, there was no other way out besides the door we had been so rudely pushed through, nor were there any windows. It also appeared to be more stoutly constructed than the front room.

It was bare of any furnishings, but before the match burned down to Poudlum's finger tips and he had to shake it out, I saw the outline of some boxes or cartons stacked against the back wall.

"You see that?" Poudlum said as he blew on his finger-tips.

"Yeah, what you think it is?"

"I'll strike another match and we'll see," he said.

"Wait a minute, how many matches you got left?"

"Maybe a dozen or so."

"Too bad we don't have something to light so we don't have to use up our matches."

"I know what we can do," Poudlum said.

"What?"

"Old Dudley ain't as smart as the bank robbers were."

"What do you mean?" I asked.

"He didn't take our pocket knives. What I can do is carve out a good long splinter from the floor, light it, and it'll burn long enough so we can see what this room looks like, and what's in them boxes. Just hold on, I can do it by feel."

I heard the metallic click as Poudlum opened his Barlow.

"What I'll do is carve two good-sized notches in the edge of this board, and then I'll put the blade of my knife into one of 'em and slide it down to the other one."

"Be careful," I told him. "Don't cut yourself."

"Only thing gonna get cut is old Dudley's nose if he sticks his head through that door."

In a few moments, I heard the cracking sound as Poudlum pried the splinter loose from the board.

"Here, you take it while I strike another match," he told me.

We fumbled through the darkness and made the transfer. Then Poudlum struck another match. It flamed up and he held it to the end of the splinter. It sputtered to life like some kind of miniature torch. I held it overhead and we turned toward the far wall and the boxes.

The splinter cast an eerie light about the dark room as it flickered and sputtered.

There were about a dozen boxes, and as I held the light, Poudlum opened the top one, reached inside and pulled out a quart fruit jar. When he screwed the lid off of it, we could smell the strong odor of alcohol.

"White lightning!" Poudlum said. "Looks like we done found ourselves another bootlegger!"

"We got to figure out a way to get out of here," I said as Poudlum was replacing the illegal whiskey.

"We'll cut our way out," he said.

"How in the world we gonna do that?"

"With our knives. Hold the light down close to the floor. There! See the nail heads where the board is nailed to the beam underneath it?"

"Yeah, I see 'em."

Poudlum asked me to move the light down the board a little ways. "Stop right there!" he said. "There's the nail heads in the next beam. Let me mark the spot with my knife."

I watched as he marked the spots between the beams by cutting a big notch at each starting point. "It's going to take a lot of whittling to cut through that heavy board with only our pocket knives," I surmised.

"Got any better ideas?" Poudlum asked.

"Nope. Let's commence to whittling. I think we can do it in the dark after we get started. That way we can both work at the same time."

Poudlum got a good v-shaped wedge started and then held our little torch while I did the same at the other end.

Then I spit on the dying embers of our torch to make sure it was completely out, and we went to work in the dark with our knives.

It wasn't long before I felt my blade cut through the board. Then I folded it back into the case and opened the middle-sized blade.

After I had about a half-inch cut in the board, I asked Poudlum how long he thought it would take us to cut it all the way through.

"How long you think we been at it?" he asked.

"It's been a good twenty minutes, maybe thirty."

"Judging from what I done cut and feeling across the rest of the board, I figure it'll take us another two hours at least, and that's if we keep steady at it."

"Good," I said. "That way we can sneak on out of here right after dark."

"We might not have to cut it clean through. Maybe we'll be able to stomp on it and break it out when we get over halfway."

"I think my knife's getting dull, Poudlum."

"Here, take my whetrock and sharpen it up. While you're at that, I'll see if I can slice a splinter out of this board from my end to yours."

I could hear Poudlum grunting and working the blade of his knife while I scraped the blade of my own across the little flat stone.

In a few moments I heard a slight cracking sound as he pried out the splinter from the edge of the board, and lo and behold, a little sliver of light came filtering up from underneath the house.

"Look at that!" Poudlum whispered excitedly. "That's enough light to really see how to cut. We won't need no more fire, which is fine with me, because it made me nervous having a flame around all that shine. One mistake and it would blow us to kingdom come."

As we cut deeper and deeper into the board, Poudlum kept slicing splinters from it lengthwise. By the time it looked like it was beginning to get dusk dark outside, we were only about two-thirds of the way through.

We had both developed blisters on our hands and that had slowed us considerably. "My hand aches something awful, Poudlum, and I can't hardly find a way to turn my fingers where there ain't a blister."

"Mine, too," he said. "But I got an idea."

"What is it?"

"We could just finish cutting it through on one end and it would be easy to just break the other end. I'm gonna cut a piece off the tail of my shirt to wrap my hand in. If you'll just keep me a sharp knife ready, I'll have this sucker cut through in another thirty minutes."

"I would sure hate for them to come busting in here and catch us after we done gone to all this work," I told Poudlum while I was sharpening his knife and he was using mine.

He stopped with the knife for a moment and looked at the door to the front room and asked, "Didn't that door open into this room?"

"Yeah, I believe it did. Why?"

"They must be fifteen or twenty cases of whiskey over there. If we walked real soft-like and stacked it all against the door, they couldn't get in here so easy."

"Good idea! I'll get right to it."

"By the time you get 'em all moved over there, I should have this board just about ready to bust out."

I walked soft as a cat, found the squeaky spots and remembered to avoid them as I made sixteen round trips across the floor. I was surprised at how heavy the cases were, but I discovered each one contained twelve quarts, which was equal to three gallons.

When I finished, I had transported forty-eight gallons of moonshine and had it snuggled up against the door, and I knew it would take a mighty shove to open it, especially if we added our weight to it.

After I returned to Poudlum's side, I saw he only lacked about a quarter of an inch before it looked like we might be able to break the floorboard out. It was at that moment we heard the ruckus up front. We froze for a moment, then tiptoed over to the wall and placed our ears against it.

Silas had come back, and he was yelling at Dudley, "You dumb idiot! I told you not to let them boys leave—"

"But-but-but, Silas," Dudley interrupted with a stutter. "I never did!"

"Then where in the dickens are they, you blubbering hunk of lard!"

"I got 'em shut up in the shine room."

"Why did you put 'em in there?"

"It was the only way I could keep them from trying to leave."

"Well, they better be in there, 'cause if they ain't we done lost two hundred dollars, and I will have to take it out of your hide."

Poudlum leaned over and whispered to me, "What you think he meant by saying he would lose two hundred dollars if we ain't in here?"

"I don't know. Listen!" I said as the conversation on the other side of the door began again.

Silas was yelling at Dudley again. "Look at this mess, empty cans everywhere. Why you done eat every morsel of food them boys brought with 'em and I was counting on that to feed 'em on the way down the river to Mobile."

Poudlum poked me and said, "You hear what he said? I better get back to cutting that board!"

"You think we could break it out right now if we had to?"

"We might be able to."

"Then let's listen a little bit more."

"How did you get 'em to go in the shine room?" Silas was asking.

"I tricked 'em," Dudley said boastfully.

"You tricked 'em?" Silas said as he roared with laughter. "You ain't never tricked nobody about nothing."

"Well, I did them," Dudley said.

"How did you do it?'

"I just made like it was the back door to the house and not to the shine room. When they opened it and poked they heads in, I give 'em a shove, slammed the door, and dropped the latch."

"You better not have hurt either one of them. Mr. Kim don't like damaged goods."

"What's Mr. Kim gonna do with 'em?" Dudley asked.

"He takes 'em to some of his friends he knows who are

in charge of big freight ships fixin' to go to China."

"What they do with the boys on the ships?"

"They use 'em as cabin boys."

"What do a cabin boy do?" Dudley asked.

"They do things like serve the captain his meals, shine his shoes, and I don't know what all."

"I kind of hate to think about them two boys getting sent all the way over to China and never seein' they kinfolks again."

"Don't you go gittin' soft on me, Dudley. That two hundred dollars is gonna set us up somewhere on a bayou down there, and we'll be eatin' shrimp and oysters instead of catfish all the time. I been waitin' on a opportunity like this for quite a spell, then that storm blew 'em right into our hands."

Poudlum grabbed me by the shirt and whispered, "They worse than the Klan! Gonna sell us into slavery to some Chinese folks. Let's bust on out of here right now!"

I started to move away from the wall with Poudlum when we heard Silas say, "We need to feed 'em somethin'. Open the door real careful and give 'em a couple of biscuits while I hold my pistol on 'em."

"He's got a gun!" Poudlum hissed.

"All the more reason to skedaddle right now! Come on!" I said.

I lingered for another moment and heard Dudley say, "Them biscuits is cold, left from this morning. Let me fix 'em somethin' hot."

"All right," Silas said. "Scramble up some eggs for 'em."

We had a reprieve, at least for a few minutes, so we tiptoed back over to the hole we were cutting. It had gotten dark outside, and once again we had to work in the dark.

"Let's both get a real good grip and see if we can rip it on out," Poudlum suggested.

We planted our feet on the floor, grasped the board with both hands, put our backs into it and pulled, but the tough old pine board just wouldn't break off.

Before I could say what next, Poudlum had dropped to his knees and was frantically cutting at the board with his knife again.

"Shore would like some of them scrambled eggs," he said as he attacked the board. "But I don't plan on waiting around for 'em."

"Me, neither," I told him as I took the whetrock out and began sharpening the big blade of my knife. About every thirty seconds Poudlum would pass me a dull knife, and I would pass him a sharp one.

I was beginning to suspect we weren't going to be able to get the board out of the floor and escape before they attempted to bring us some food, and it turned out I was correct.

Suddenly, there was a pounding on the door, and Silas yelled out, "We fixin' to bring you boys some supper. When Dudley opens that door, y'all best stay back so you don't get hurt."

There was a brief silence before Dudley said, "They ain't answering."

"I know that. Don't you think I can hear?" Silas scolded. "Just set they plates on the floor and open the door."

"Here they come, Poudlum!" I said.

"The stack of shine will hold 'em for a while," he reassured me. "We gonna make it. I think in just a little bit we can both stomp on the board, and it'll break down easier than if we pull up on it."

We heard a thud on the door.

"Well, open the door," Silas yelled.

"It won't open," Dudley told him.

"What you mean it won't open?"

"They is something holding it."

I heard some more bumping and knocking around the door, and then we heard Silas yell, "They done stacked the shine against the door! Come on, Dudley, and help me push!"

When I looked toward the door I saw the dark mound of illegal whiskey move ever so slightly.

Chapter 12

The Escape

I leaned over my shoulder and called out to Poudlum, "They gonna push their way in!"

"Push back and just give me one more minute," he said.

I felt the stack of moonshine move toward me when I leaned against it and saw a thin frame of light around the top of the door. With my back to the boxes and my feet planted on the floor, I pushed back as hard as I could and momentarily felt the movement toward me slacken.

"Push harder!" I heard Silas yell from the other side of the door, and a moment later I could tell they had redoubled their efforts, and when I looked up I saw the crack at the top of the door was now an inch wide.

"I can't hold 'em much longer, Poudlum!" I whispered as loud as I could through my clenched teeth.

"No need to!" Poudlum said right after I heard a loud cracking sound. "I just stomped the board out. Let's go!"

When I got to the hole in the floor, Poudlum's head was disappearing through it. "Come on," he called out to me from underneath the floor.

As I dropped my feet through the hole, the big stack of moonshine came crashing down. When the top case hit the floor, a quart jar flew out, took one bounce and burst. I felt the spray and bits of broken glass hit my face as I slipped through and disappeared beneath the floor where Poudlum was on his hand and knees waiting on me.

We had to stay low to keep from bumping our heads as we crawled toward the outside. The last thing I heard from above was a lot of thumping, bumping, crashing, and cussing.

When we cleared the edge of the floor and stood up outside, Poudlum said, "They gonna be mad as two old wet hens!"

"I hope they drown in all that whiskey," I told him as we broke into a run toward the river.

When we reached the river's edge, we were mighty grateful to find our boat beached there. We never broke stride as we shoved her into the water and leapt aboard, where the paddles and the rest of our stuff was secure except our blankets and our food store.

As we dug our paddles deep into the water and pulled away, we heard our former hosts yelling as they ran to the water's edge, but we were gone into the darkness and safety of the river.

The current had subsided, but it was still difficult paddling upstream. When I moved back from the bow of the boat to sit across from Poudlum, I stumbled over something. When I investigated it with my hands, it turned out to be a half-empty box with six quarts of moonshine in it.

When I got Poudlum to feel it and identify it, he said,

"It appears Silas been out delivering shine in our boat."

We took the lids off the jars and poured the strong-smelling contents into the river, leaned over the side of the boat, rinsed out the jars, and stowed them away. After that, we relaxed some as we were well away from our captors. The dim light of their shack disappeared as we paddled on up the river.

"You think it rained while we was sleeping or locked up in that room?" Poudlum asked.

"I don't think so," I told him and then asked why he had asked.

"Because there's about a inch of water in the bottom of the boat," he answered.

We were fortunate that two of our torches were still in the boat and had dried out. Poudlum lit one while I paddled and began to inspect the inside of the boat.

A few moments later I heard him say, "Uh oh!"

"What's the matter?" I asked.

"We got a hole in our boat!"

"What?! How big is it?"

"Big enough. Looks about the size of a bullet hole, but water's gurgling up through it. Looks like we got two or three inches in the bottom. We got to get off the river!"

"Can we make it to the other side?"

"We ought to be able to. You paddle and I'll start bailing."

Before he grabbed the bailing bucket, Poudlum propped our torch up like a beacon in the front of the boat. It gave us enough light to see how to get to the far side of the river. Now all we had to do was find a good spot to land.

I turned the boat and headed her straight across the river toward the far shoreline. When we got there, we saw it was dark with overhanging bushes and no place to land because the river was still about two feet higher than normal.

"Better find a spot quick 'cause this water is gaining on me!" Poudlum told me.

I knew he was right because I could feel the water creeping into my shoes, and the boat was responding more and more sluggishly.

I looked down and saw the reflection of the flickering torch on the water gathering in the bottom of the boat.

"Better stop paddling and help me bail unless you want to swim," Poudlum said as he slung a bucket of water overboard.

"I got a better idea," I told him.

"Better make it quick."

"Blow the torch out and then get low in the boat. I'm gonna crash us into the brush. When we hit it grab whatever you can and pull us toward the shore."

We hit with a soft crash, and in the darkness, we reached out and grabbed overhanging limbs and pulled with all our might. When we touched bottom, we reached farther toward the shore and clutched at others. Finally, we heard a grinding sound, and the boat came to a halt.

"Feels like we made it to shore," Poudlum said.

"You think you can light that torch again?" I asked.

Poudlum struck a match on his belt buckle and reignited our pine torch. We looked around and saw we had landed on a fairly steep grade and up ahead was a giant oak tree with wide sweeping branches, some of which we had used to pull ourselves ashore. When we investigated further, we found that underneath the majestic tree trunk there was a natural clearing which appeared very inviting.

"First thing we got to do is drag the boat up on dry land or we might lose her," Poudlum said.

We pushed the bottom end of the torch into the soft ground and used the light of it to wrap a rope around the mighty tree trunk and drag our boat out of the water. We still had our ax, cooking and fishing gear, and the tarp, which we transferred up underneath the big tree. After that, we pushed and shoved until we got the boat in a position so the hole was downhill to allow all the water to drain out of it.

"Next thing we need is a fire," Poudlum said.

"We gonna be hard pressed to find any dry wood," I told him. "Everything is still wet after all the rain."

"We won't mess with any hardwood then," he said. "We'll just collect the heart of some rotten pine trees. It'll be damp but we can get it started with the torch," Poudlum reassured me.

So we ventured out into the forest with me holding the torch and Poudlum wielding the ax. Within a matter of minutes, we had dragged several hearts of pine trees underneath the big tree where Poudlum chopped them into pieces, and we soon had a nice fire going.

And of course, while knocking the rotten wood off the heart of the pine trees, Poudlum had collected an ample supply of grub worms and deposited them into one of Silas's moonshine jars, and while I held the torch, we returned to the water and set out some lines suspended from the low limbs of our giant tree.

When we retuned to our fire, we became aware of what a magnificent spot we had accidentally crashed into. The giant tree with its huge drooping branches was like an umbrella of nature and gave the impression we had a leafy mansion over our heads. Long gray tentacles of Spanish moss hung from the limbs, which we gathered for our beds.

Afterwards, we folded the dry side of the tarp up and made ourselves a giant hammock, which we hung from two big low limbs, and used some of our rope to secure the four corners. Then we placed the big pile of moss inside of it, and we had ourselves a nice place to sleep.

But there was something else really bothering us. It was hunger. We hadn't had a bite to eat since the night before.

"I don't never 'member being so hungry," Poudlum said. "My stomach is rubbing against my backbone. Right now I would gladly let myself be sold off as a slave to some Chinese man just for some of Dudley's scrambled eggs."

"It wasn't just our food; we lost our blankets, too," I lamented.

"Fire's going good," Poudlum said. "Let's go check them lines. Maybe we got lucky."

We lit another torch and went to the water's edge only to find that our lines hung limp and our hooks bare. Poudlum put some fresh bait on the hooks, and we returned to our fire in a sad and hungry state.

To keep our minds off food, we decided to see if we could repair our boat. After we dragged it up next to our fire, we flipped it over so we could examine the hole in it.

"What I figure," Poudlum surmised, "is that Silas was

out peddling his whiskey, got into some kind of ruckus, probably from cheating somebody, and got shot at."

"Sounds likely. You think we can fix it?" I asked.

"Maybe we could hammer a fishing cork into it to hold it for a while. Would you fetch me one from our fishing gear?" Poudlum asked as he continued to inspect the hole.

I watched as he whittled the stubby end of a cork down so it would fit. Then he took the head of our ax and hammered it into the hole until it was so tight we couldn't budge it with our hands.

"All right," he said. "At least we can get out on the river again and find us some food in the morning; that is, if we don't starve to death tonight."

"Good work, Poudlum," I told him. "Why don't you go check the lines again, and I'll stoke up the fire and heat up some grease just in case."

I had the fire going good with lots of hot coals, and as I sat there contemplating how we were going to sleep through the night being so hungry, a wonderful sight emerged from the darkness into the circle of light from the fire.

It was Poudlum with a whopper in each hand. He had a finger from each hand hooked into the mouths and out of the gills of two big cats with their whiskers still quivering and their tails still flipping.

I got the grease good and hot while Poudlum dressed them out. Our salt and meal were both a little soggy, but we managed, and before long we were feasting on fresh, sweet fish, and even had enough to save some for the next morning.

Later on, with full bellies, we snuggled into our bed

of soft moss suspended above the ground while the fire crackled softly below us, and the faint swishing sound of the river came filtering through the tree branches as we reflected on our good fortune.

"Ain't this something?" Poudlum said. "We been chased up and down the river by the Klan, caught in a flood, locked up by bootleggers, almost sold off as slaves and shipped off to China, had our boat almost sink, about starved to death, and just look at us now. Here we are free as birds, safe and sound, warm and comfortable with full bellies."

"I guess we just two lucky boys, Poudlum."

"Naw, it ain't just that," he said.

"What else?" I asked.

"I'll tell you what I think."

"Well, go ahead and tell me then," I told him.

"I think the good Lord looks after the birds and the squirrels, and surely, he's gonna look after us."

After contemplating what Poudlum had said, I told him I thought he was right.

IT TURNED OUT TO be the best night's sleep we had had since we had been on the river.

When I woke up, I rolled to the edge of our makeshift hammock and saw Poudlum bent over the ashes of last night's fire, attempting to bring it back to life.

He blew away the gray ashes, and I saw live coals underneath. He layered some of our Spanish moss on top of the glowing coals and continued blowing. Suddenly the flames leapt to life, and he added more fuel to it and before I could get my feet on the ground, he had a nice fire going.

"You don't reckon anybody will see the smoke, do you?"

"Not after it filters up through this big old tree," I told him.

We had two thick slabs of fish left. We shared one for breakfast and saved the other one for lunch.

After that, we used the bailing bucket to haul water up from the river. We heated the water on our fire and bathed ourselves and put on fresh shirts and pants. We found a spring back into the woods aways, drank our fill, and filled our water jug from it.

Now that we were rested, clean, and fed, we were ready to take on the world again.

It was getting on toward mid-morning when we ventured down, parted the tree branches, and peered out upon the river. The water had receded to normal level, and the river was like a field of jewels as the warm sunshine glinted and bounced across it.

We looked up and down the river and saw it was deserted, and retreated back to our giant tree sanctuary to contemplate our next move.

As we folded the tarp, we kept our moss inside it. When we had it good and tight, we tied a piece of rope around it, and Poudlum said, "What you think we ought to do?"

"I don't think anybody crossed the river yesterday. Mr. Henry wouldn't have taken his ferry out in that current, but everything looks normal today."

"So you think Mr. Curvin will finally come back from Choctaw County?"

"Uh-huh, and Mr. Henry will tell him what's been going

on and tell him we planned to paddle down to the Jackson Bridge and meet him there."

We flipped the boat over, loaded it up and began dragging it toward the water. But just before we reached the water's edge, we peeked through the branches one more time, and what we saw caused us to retreat quickly back into them.

Chapter 13

Mr. Kim

It was Silas and a Chinese-looking man in a large boat. It had a motor on it, but they were paddling very deliberately, and they were right on top of us when we first saw them. However, as a result of our good hiding place, they hadn't seen us as we observed them.

The Chinese man wore a loose black shirt, and his hair was in a long plait down his back. Below his cold eyes, a long, thin, and limp moustache drooped over the corners of his mouth.

"That must be Mr. Kim," Poudlum whispered. "The one who wanted to buy us for two hundred dollars and make us into ship slaves."

"I think you are right about that," I whispered back. "Silas don't look too happy about losing his investment, either."

We continued conversing in whispers because we knew how sound carried better over water than it did over land.

"They are definitely looking for us," I said. "See how they're looking for a landing spot on the bank?"

"Uh-huh, and if we had found us a nice clear spot to

land instead of crashing into these thick limbs, they probably would've found us. Like I told you, the Good Lord is looking out for us."

We watched until they disappeared around the next bend in the river. Then we retreated back to our sanctuary under the giant tree, where we sat down and leaned our backs against its massive trunk while we contemplated our situation.

"This mess we in reminds me of one of my momma's favorite sayings," Poudlum said.

"What's that?"

"I believe we are in between the devil and the deep blue sea, but in this case, between the devil and the river."

"How's that?" I asked.

"The Klan's looking for us upriver, and the slavers are looking for us downriver."

"You know what, Poudlum?"

"What?"

"That does ring true if you consider the Klan to be the devil and the slavers to be the deep blue sea."

"So what we gonna do?"

"Well, it's for sure we can't paddle up to Jackson in the daylight. If we take to the water, it'll have to be after dark."

"We could just take to the woods and walk up to Jackson," Poudlum suggested.

"I guess we could, but what if it got dark on us before we there? I would hate to be caught out in the deep woods at night. Plus there's probably a lot of swamps between here and there. And if we had to spend the night in the woods, how would we know which way to go in the morning?"

"Okay," Poudlum said. "Forget traveling through the woods and the swamps. Probably a lot of quicksand and snakes in them swamps. We best stick to the river."

"I think you are right, Poudlum. Remember, we don't have any food, and at least here on the river, we can get fish to eat."

"Speaking of that," Poudlum said. "We better go bait and set out some lines since we gonna be here until after dark."

While we were setting lines out to catch us some dinner, it occurred to me that if we didn't show up at Jackson today, my uncle would probably sound the alarm, and folks would start looking for us.

When I told Poudlum this, he said, "You think they'll think we drowned and go out on the water and fire cannons to see if our bodies will float up like they did when Huck Finn disappeared?"

We had both recently finished reading *The Adventures of Tom Sawyer* and *Adventures of Huckleberry Finn*, which my brother Fred had given to us as gifts. I read one and Poudlum read the other, and then we traded.

"I doubt if they'll do that, but by the time dark comes tonight and we don't show up, I'll guarantee Uncle Curvin will have a lot of folks out on the river looking for us tomorrow."

Poudlum sighed and said, "That means we got to hide out till then with nothing to eat."

"We can get fish," I told him.

"You know what?" he said.

"What?"

"I never thought I would live to say it, but I'm about done got myself a bait of catfish."

"What! You don't want no more catfish?"

"Oh, I'll eat it and be thankful for it, but I got myself a hankering for some fried chicken, mashed taters, and some fried okra."

"I know what you mean," I told Poudlum as my mouth watered thinking about the food he had mentioned.

When midday came, we shared the last piece of fish from last night, and it was still tasty even though we were tired of it. Just before dusk dark, we made a small fire and fried up our catch of the day, enough to last us another day. I fanned the smoke to spread it out while Poudlum did the cooking.

We let our fire die out and sat in the darkness until the moon appeared. The full one had gone, and all the sky could boast of was a dim crescent moon.

It was darker than it had been on the previous nights on the river, but we managed to get our boat in the water in the dimness and began paddling upstream toward Jackson.

"What we gonna do when we get to the bridge?" Poudlum asked.

"I think we ought to hide in the woods in sight of the bridge, and when we see Uncle Curvin, make a break for it."

"That sounds good to me," Poudlum said as we dug our paddles deep.

It was only a moment after Poudlum said, "We ought to

get there before daylight," when a false daylight suddenly descended upon us.

We froze when the light hit us and illuminated our boat and the river around us. We were shocked into inaction, and before we could react, Silas and Mr. Kim's boat collided with ours while they held a carbide lantern on our faces.

"Hey, boys," Silas said gleefully. "Glad to see y'all again. It hurt my feelings that y'all left in such a hurry, 'specially after I took the two of you in after the storm."

Before we could react in any way, they grabbed the side of our boat, and Mr. Kim stepped aboard with a rope and lashed it to our boat.

He never said a word. Silas did all the talking. "We gonna take you boys down the river a ways and introduce you to some friends who want to take y'all on a real long trip, but first we gonna make a quick stop by my place. Now y'all just sit still while we get our motor started."

Poudlum and I were in shock, and before we could dive overboard, Mr. Kim had our hands and feet tied.

I felt helpless as Silas started the motor, turned us back downstream and began speeding away toward our proposed enslavement.

With their boat in front and ours tied behind, the wind hit us squarely in our helpless faces as we sped downriver toward unknown horrors.

Before we got back to Silas's cabin, I managed to work my knife out of my pocket and slip it inside of my sock.

Their motor slacked off, and it wasn't long before we slid onto the landing at the familiar site of Silas and Dudley's place.

They loosened the bonds on our feet and led us up the shore and back into the cabin we had escaped from the night before.

Dudley stared at us with his dull eyes like he was mad with us for escaping. He shoved us against the wall and finally said in a gruff tone, "Y'all sit down there and keep your traps shut."

Silas and Mr. Kim went into the back room and started hauling boxes of whiskey out and stacking them on the front porch.

After several trips Silas stepped back inside, stopped in front of us, looked down and said, "You young rascals cost me some money. We lost six quarts of shine when that stack y'all made got pushed over. That's all right though; I'll get it back plus a lot more when we get downriver."

Then he turned to Dudley and said, "Me and Mr. Kim got to deliver the rest of this shine. We'll be back by dawn. You let these boys get away again, and I'll skin you alive. Soon as we get back, we'll be heading down the river for good."

Mr. Kim never spoke at all. He did his talking with his eyes as he gave us a piercing and threatening look before he walked out the door with Silas.

The shock of our capture had dissipated, and Poudlum and I were talking with our eyes also, while Dudley sat there slack-jawed staring at us.

Now it was just us and Dudley, and I could tell by the look in Poudlum's eyes that he was formulating a plan to outwit him.

"Y'all think you real smart, don't you?" Dudley said.

"Busting out of here like y'all did. It made me look real bad, and got Silas real mad with me."

Poudlum spoke first. "It wasn't your fault, Dudley. It was Silas's fault for not taking our knives away from us."

Dudley looked at me and said, "How come yore little colored friend is talkin' like a white person?"

Poudlum answered for me. "You wants me to talk like a colored person, Dudley. I will if you wants me to. I'll say dis and dat and dem and dose if you wants me to, 'cause I speaks two languages."

Dudley was dumbfounded by what Poudlum said, but I knew Poudlum was just trying to get him bumfuzzled.

Now it was my turn. "We awful hungry, Dudley. You think we could have some beans and sardines from the food we left here?"

He lowered his eyes in shame and said, "I done et up all that stuff."

"Well, do you have anything to eat?" I asked him.

"All I got is some biscuits and some side meat," he said.

"Hey, that sounds mighty good. You think we could have a bite? We ain't had nothing to eat for two days," I lied.

"I reckon it'll be all right to give y'all a biscuit," he conceded.

"Well, we can't eat with our hands tied."

"All right, I'll untie yo' hands so you can eat, but I'll do it one at a time. First y'all stand up so I can take them knives off you."

I stood up first, and Dudley went through my pockets before asking, "Where's that pocket knife?"

"I think I lost it cleaning fish," I lied again.

After Dudley untied my hands but not my feet, he brought me a biscuit with a slice of side meat in it, and it was mighty tasty.

When he had retied my hands, he ordered Poudlum to stand up, after which he removed his Barlow and a little snuff can from his pockets and placed them on the table.

"You know you too young to be dipping snuff, boy," Dudley lectured him.

"I reckon you right, Dudley, but I sure do love my snuff."

After Poudlum had eaten his biscuit, Dudley told him to turn around so he could retie his hands.

"I really do enjoy a good dip of snuff after my meal, Dudley. Do you mind if I get myself a dip before you tie me back up?"

"I don't reckon I see no harm in that," Dudley said as he handed Poudlum the snuff can.

I watched as Poudlum carefully removed the lid from the can and opened his mouth like he was going to take a dip. Then in one swift motion, he slung the little can of ground-up red peppers into Dudley's face.

I was astounded at the effect it had on him. He took a tremendous intake of breath, which was the worst thing he could have done. Then he screamed and clutched at his eyes before he staggered backwards, crashed into the wall and fell to the floor. The screaming turned into choking and gagging sounds as he lay there jerking and twisting, first rubbing his eyes, then grabbing at his throat.

Meanwhile, Poudlum hadn't wasted any time. By the

time Dudley had hit the floor, he had gotten busy at untying his feet, and now he was loosening the ropes on my hands.

"Oh, Lord, y'all done kilt me," Dudley moaned

"You ain't gonna die, Dudley," Poudlum called out over his shoulder as he finished untying me.

"Good move!" I told him.

"I knew that pepper would come in handy one day. When you finish untying your feet bring the rope over so we can tie Dudley up."

"I'm blinded!" Dudley called out in agony as he groped about and attempted to sit up.

"You'll be able to see again if you listen to me," Poudlum told him.

"Oh yes, I'll listen," Dudley whimpered. "Please get me some water."

"Got to tie you up first. Stick your hands out in front of yourself."

I went out on the porch to get a bucket of water and the dipper when I saw Poudlum was well along into tying up a defeated Dudley. While I was out there, I looked down toward the dark edge of the river, and I could see the dim outline of our boat, our vehicle of escape.

When I got back inside, Poudlum had Dudley propped up against the wall and was binding his ankles while he continued to blubber and blink his red and swollen eyes. When Poudlum finished, he tied another length of rope from his feet and secured it up over a rafter so Dudley couldn't crawl outside.

Then I held the bucket while Poudlum took a dipper

full of water and dashed it into Dudley's face.

"Oh, bless you, bless you!" Dudley sputtered. "Do it again, please."

After another dipper full in the face from Poudlum, I took a full dipper and held it to his lips and watched him guzzle it down like a thirsty mule.

When I looked up, I saw Poudlum placing slices of side meat into several biscuits, which he jammed into a brown paper bag before rolling down the top.

I gathered up our blankets, and we headed for the door. Just as we got to it, Dudley called out, "Y'all know Silas and Mr. Kim is gonna kill me, don't you?"

I found myself feeling sorry for him, all hogtied up there on the floor, still blubbering, so I told him, "Just tell 'em several of our friends busted in and overpowered you."

Poudlum added, "Tell 'em they'll be waiting outside for them, too. And one other thing, Dudley, if you make a sound we'll come back in here and give you another dose of that snuff."

With that, we dashed out the door, ran across the porch and hit the ground running. When we got to the river, we tossed the biscuits and our blankets in our boat.

As we were just about ready to launch the boat, Poudlum said, "You know, we could run into 'em again, and they could chase us down with their motor."

"Hold on then," I told him. "I think I got a better idea!"

Chapter 14

The Wicked Knife

"What you got in mind?" Poudlum asked as we momentarily ceased our efforts to push our boat into the water.

"I don't think we ought to take the chance of going back out on the river with them having the advantage of a motor on their boat. I don't doubt we could outpaddle them, but we can't outpaddle a motor."

"But what else can we do? We got to at least get across the river."

"Silas said they would be back by dawn from their whiskey-running. If they see our boat is gone, they gonna know at once we done got away, and they'll start looking for us. But if our boat is still here, they'll think we're still tied up inside with Dudley."

"But if our boat is still here, then we will be, too," Poudlum reminded me.

"That's right. What we could do is hide out and take both boats when they get up to the cabin, and that way they wouldn't have no way to chase us."

"We would have to move real fast," Poudlum warned.

"It do sound like a good plan, but we better work out the details, and work them out good."

"All right, let's get started."

The first thing we did was retie the rope which secured our boat and put a slipknot in it so all we would have to do was give the loose end of the rope a yank to free it.

Essentially, our plan was to tie our boat to the back of theirs as soon as they disembarked and began walking toward the cabin. Once that was done we intended to rapidly launch their boat, start the motor and race away before they could get back down to the river after they discovered we had outwitted and overcome Dudley.

"You don't think it might be stealing to take their boat, do you?" Poudlum asked.

"No, because we'll be taking it from bootleggers and kidnappers."

"I reckon I have to agree with that. But where we gonna hide out till they get here? It's got to be somewhere close by, but we don't want to be staying in the water that long."

"Yeah, it's got to be somewhere besides the water," I agreed.

There was a big bushy oak tree nearby with branches low enough so we could reach up and grab them. When I proposed it as a hiding place, Poudlum readily agreed and said, "That tree is about the only hiding place close enough for our plan to work, but it might be a little uncomfortable being up there till daylight."

"It must be about midnight," I said. "We'll stay on the ground until the last hour or two before dawn."

We agreed that one of us should stay awake the rest of

the night, and we would take turns being on watch. We devised a method of keeping up with the time by using pebbles, which we scooped up from the edge of the river. They were white and shiny and the moon gave off just enough light to see them and count them.

I took the first two-hour shift while Poudlum took his blanket from the boat, rolled up in it, and went right off to sleep.

To count the minutes and the hours, I took a pebble from the pile and put it in a new pile every time I counted to sixty, representing one minute. When I had sixty pebbles transferred to the new pile, I knew an hour had passed. Then I did it all over again, and when I had 120 pebbles in the new pile, I knew two hours had passed, and it was time to wake up Poudlum.

I gently awakened Poudlum for his two-hour shift. Once I got him fully awake, I showed him my pile of 120 pebbles, which he could discard one by one and then wake me up when they were all gone, which should be about four o'clock in the morning.

I rolled up in his still-warm blanket and went right off to sleep. It seemed like I had just closed my eyes when I felt him gently shaking my shoulder and whispering, "Wake up. It ought not to be but a hour or two before daylight."

We had agreed to spend the last watch up in the tree with both of us staying awake, so after we had reviewed our plan and walked through it two times, we put the blanket back into our boat and approached the tree. It was only about twenty yards from the boat landing, and we judged the cabin to be about a hundred, so we felt comfortable it would work.

There was nothing difficult about getting up in the tree. We just had to reach up and grasp a massive limb and pull ourselves up. We climbed to the second row of limbs and nestled our backs up against the trunk of the tree and rested our legs on the limbs, which were thicker than our bodies.

From our perches, we were making sure we could see the boat and the shore of the river when Poudlum said, "You remember the last time we was up a tree together?"

"Yeah, it was when that big mean bulldog had us treed."

"Jake ain't gonna show up to save us this time," he said. "We'll have to do it ourselves."

"We can," I reassured him. "All we got to do is stick to our plan and execute it."

"I feel like a panther laying up here in this tree waiting for my quarry to pass underneath so I can pounce down on it," Poudlum mused.

"Yeah, but instead of a deer or a rabbit, our quarry is them two boats."

Things were so still and quiet we could barely hear anything except the movement of the river, and barely that. My eyes got so heavy it felt like I needed some fence posts to keep them propped open. I shook my head to drive the drowsiness away and asked Poudlum how long he thought it was before daylight.

The only response I got was a soft snore.

I reached over and shook his shoulder and said, "Wake up, Poudlum. We can't go to sleep now!"

"Huh?" he responded.

"A sleeping panther will let his quarry pass by unmolested. We got to stay awake. It ought not to be too long now."

When a faint light began to sift through the trees from the east, and the frogs began to croak, I knew it truly wouldn't be long before daylight.

Suddenly, Poudlum said, "You hear that?"

"What?"

"Listen."

I cocked my head, listened intently, and in between the sound of the toads toasting the dawn, I heard the faint sound of a boat motor.

"It's them!" I said.

Way out on the river, a dim light appeared and increased with the sound of the motor as Silas's and Mr. Kim's boat approached the bank.

We instinctively scrunched up a little closer to the trunk of the tree when we heard them cut the motor off. We also heard the sound of the boat as its momentum caused it to slide halfway up on the low bank of the river.

As the two of them stepped out of the boat and onto the bank, Silas spoke first. His wicked words came drifting up through the foliage when he said to Mr. Kim, "Let's go get yo' two cabin boys and get on down the river."

Mr. Kim didn't say anything. He just moved slowly and deliberately as if he had some kind of sinister purpose in mind.

"I'm stiff as a board," Silas said as he put his hand on his hips and stretched his back.

It wasn't quite daylight yet, but there was enough gray

light so that objects had begun to take form, and that was almost our undoing.

Silas took two steps before stopping in his tracks and casting his carbide lamp into our boat. "Wait a minute," he said. "Them blankets wasn't in that boat when we left."

My heart began pounding like a drum, and I felt Poudlum's grip on my arm as we pressed back against the tree trunk, wishing we could sink into the very bark of it.

"Should've left while we could," Poudlum whispered.

Then we breathed a heavy sigh of relief when Silas said, "Dudley must have already started loading up. Come on, Mr. Kim." Then he turned and began walking toward the cabin. "I saved one case of shine for you. I'll wager it tastes a lot better than that sour stuff you fellows brew out of rice."

We relinquished our grips on the tree slightly as they began walking away. That is until we saw the horrible deed that happened next.

With Silas one step ahead of him, we saw Mr. Kim pull a long shiny knife from within the folds of his long black shirt. It cast a dull glint in the early morning light.

I had to put my hand over my mouth to stifle a gasp when I saw him plunge the wicked blade into Silas's back. At first I thought I might have fallen asleep and was dreaming the grisly scene, but when I felt Poudlum's sudden grip on my shoulder and heard his sharp intake of breath, I realized the ghastly murder was really happening right before our eyes.

We watched in horror as Silas stiffened, let out a low moan, and then crumpled to the ground, after which Mr. Kim extracted his murderous blade, wiped it clean on Silas's shirt and placed it into its original hiding place.

At that moment, I almost panicked, and my muscles contracted as I thought of leaping from the tree and running away as fast as my legs would take me, but Poudlum saved me from making that fatal mistake when he whispered softly into my ear, "Don't move and don't make nary a sound."

What Mr. Kim did next revealed to us that he was not only a murderer, but also a robber. He rifled through Silas's pockets and we saw him extract a roll of folding money from the dead man's pocket and tuck it away into his own clothing.

The next thing he did was cast his eyes all around to make sure no one had seen his dastardly deed. When he began walking toward the cabin, I thanked the Good Lord he hadn't looked up.

When he was halfway there, Poudlum whispered, "Come on, we got to move!"

"I'm not sure I can," I answered.

"You got to!" Poudlum insisted as he pulled at me.

"What you think he's gonna do?" I asked.

"I expect he gonna go in the cabin, slit Dudley's throat, and come back out here looking for us."

That got me moving, and as we dropped softly from the tree and dashed to the water's edge, I asked Poudlum, "Can you start that motor?"

"No time for that!" he said as he pulled the slip knot of the rope holding our boat.

When he pushed me aboard and began casting off, I said, "But he'll catch us with that motorboat!"

"No, he won't," Poudlum said as he maneuvered our boat

to the rear of the motorboat, where I watched as he reached out and ripped the rubber gas line from the motor and held it up in his hand where it dangled like a baby snake before he tossed it into the bottom of our boat.

Just as he did that, we saw a dark figure emerge from the cabin door and onto the porch.

"Paddle like you ain't never done before!" Poudlum said as he dug his paddle deep into the water.

Mr. Kim closed the distance from the cabin to the river's edge on a dead run, but we were moving out onto the water by then.

"What if he's got a gun?" I said as I strained my muscles on the paddle.

"Don't matter if he has," Poudlum said.

"How come? He could kill us as dead as he done Silas."

"He don't want us dead," Poudlum said as he strained mightily with his paddle. "He wants us alive so he can ship us off as slaves on a slow boat to China. Paddle hard!"

Over our shoulders, we saw Mr. Kim board his boat, move to the rear of it and pull the starter rope on the motor. It sputtered and coughed but didn't fire.

He attempted to start the motor several more times to no avail, and by this time, we had put some distance between us and him.

I was beginning to feel a little relieved until I saw what he did next. I kept dedicating myself to the paddle stroke with my eyes locked on Mr. Kim. He was doing something with the motor. Then I saw him lift it out of the boat and toss it onto the bank. I knew he had realized it was useless, and he was getting rid of the weight of it.

"What's he doing?" Poudlum asked.

When I saw him grab a paddle, move to the bow of the boat and start paddling like a madman, I said, "I think he intends to chase us."

"Ain't no way he can do that," Poudlum said. "He can't outpaddle the two of us."

Poudlum and I could make a boat skim across the water, and in the last couple of days we had developed a link between us so that we both always paddled together and never against each other.

We had reached mid-river by now, and as the sun burned the remaining morning fog off, we looked back and were amazed that the space between us and Mr. Kim had not increased. He was keeping pace with us.

"That sucker can sure enough paddle," Poudlum lamented.

"Let's bear down some," I told him.

Without a starting signal, we both dug our paddles a little deeper and increased the speed of our strokes, and after about twenty minutes of this, my muscles were burning, and I had to keep wiping the sweat out of my eyes by leaning my head to either side and wiping my face on my shirt sleeves.

Sure enough, after a while, Mr. Kim had been reduced to a mere dot way back behind us.

"I guess we showed that sucker how to paddle," Poudlum said triumphantly.

"Yeah, but we can't keep this up. Let's ease up some, 'cause I'm aching all over."

So we relaxed some, paddled easily for a while, but were shocked when we looked back and saw the dot of Mr. Kim had increased into a distinguishable view of our pursuer.

"Good Lord!" Poudlum exclaimed. "That Chinese man can paddle better than I thought. We better hunker down and get back to it. Do you remember how we used to think about pleasant things when we suffered in the cotton field?"

"Uh-huh," I told him.

So we both concentrated on pleasurable things in our minds while our bodies labored over the paddles, and it soon paid off as Mr. Kim's boat once again began to recede on the horizon.

"How far you think it is up to the bridge in Jackson?" Poudlum asked in between ragged breaths.

"I think it's still a good ways up the river, 'cause we ain't even come to the place where we hid out under the big oak tree yet."

We looked back, and he was still coming, and as we tired, he slowly began to close the gap.

Once again, we dug deep into our resolve, and punished our bodies with the paddling. We did gain some distance from the man with the long thin mustache and the long sharp knife, who wanted to enslave us and ship us off to China.

We were once again maintaining our distance and were beginning to feel comfortable when suddenly a geyser erupted in the center of our boat.

Chapter 15

Running for Life

The cork Poudlum had driven into the hole in our boat had succumbed to the pressure and popped out of the hole. A fountain of river water was pouring into our boat.

Poudlum dropped his paddle and grabbed a blanket, wadded it up, and pressed down hard on the spurting fountain.

I moved to the front of the boat where I could alternate my paddle strokes on each side of the boat. Without us both paddling, our speed decreased considerably.

"You got it stopped?" I called back over my shoulder.

"I can slow it down, but I can't stop it!" he answered. "It's too much pressure pushing up! Keep paddling and when you get too tired, we'll switch places."

About ten minutes later, we made the switch, and I had to wade through several inches of water in the bottom of the boat. When I sat down and pressed the soggy blanket against the hole, I couldn't help but notice Mr. Kim was closing in on us. I kept my eyes on him while I held back the water, and it wasn't long before I knew we were in trouble because I could see the water splashing up from his paddle strokes.

"We got to head for the bank, Poudlum!"

He looked back and said, "I hope we can make it before he catches us!"

In desperation, I cast my eyes toward the eastern shore and just beyond the low growth on the bank, I saw the leafy mound of the top of the giant water oak tree we had camped under.

"There!" I pointed. "Head for the big tree!"

"I see it," Poudlum called back. "But I don't know if we can make it!"

I gauged the distance between us and Mr. Kim and the speed we were making and concluded he was right. The water in the boat was up over my ankles now, and the extra weight of it was slowing us to a crawl, which brought me to the conclusion we would be overtaken before we could reach the safety of the bank.

There was only one thing left to do. "We got to swim for it, Poudlum!"

"I heard Silas say he was gonna get two hundred dollars from that Chinese man for us. The way he's coming after us, I reckon he expects to get a lot more than that."

"I don't think he wants us for cabin boys anymore, Poudlum."

"Huh, what you mean?"

"He knows we saw him murder Silas. I know most folks would probably say he wasn't hardly worth killing, but it was murder still the same."

A shiver went through me when I heard Poudlum say,

"You're right! That's why he's coming after us so hard—he wants to get rid of the witnesses!"

"Got to leave our shoes," I told him as I ripped mine off.

"You think we can make it?" Poudlum asked as he did the same.

"We might can if we swim hard."

The last thing I heard Poudlum say before we abandoned ship was, "I know I can swim faster than we can paddle this boat."

The sinking boat lurched under us as we dived into the water. The coolness of the river actually felt good after all the hard paddling.

I surfaced, blowing water and stroking hard, with Poudlum at my side. Back over my shoulder, I could see the wispy ends of Mr. Kim's long, skinny mustache fluttering in the wind.

The shoreline was only about twenty yards away, and Mr. Kim's boat was about twice that distance behind us. Even though his boat was moving slightly faster than we were swimming, I was beginning to believe we were going to make it.

I knew we had at least made the bank when I felt the low-lying bushes on the edge brush against my face. I reached up and grabbed a strong branch and used it to pull myself up on the bank. A moment later, I reached down and pulled Poudlum up next to me.

Through the leafy branches, we saw Mr. Kim, his black shirt plastered to his body with perspiration, and a pained look in his dark eyes. He was that close, and as his boat came crashing into the underbrush, we turned and broke into a hard run.

As we raced underneath the great and beautiful tree where we had hung our hammock and slept, I heard the rattling of Mr. Kim's paddle as he dropped it in his boat.

We didn't look back for a good long spell. We just ran. We ran as hard as we had ever run in our lives. We dodged trees, leapt over dead logs, ducked under low limbs, and crashed through thickets for what seemed like an eternity.

Finally, completely exhausted, we collapsed next to a large cottonwood tree. As I lay against its smooth bark, my chest heaved, ached, and burned.

As soon as we could quiet our heavy breathing, we began to listen. We cocked our heads and listened as hard and intently as we could, and the forest was as still and quiet as a graveyard at midnight.

"How come everything is so quiet, Poudlum?" I said softly.

"Probably because of all the racket we made running. We done scared all the birds and varmints, and they doing like we doing—listening to see what they can hear."

"You think he's still coming?"

"His feet must not be touching the ground if he is, 'cause I don't hear nothing."

"Maybe we done outrun him." I said. "You think he just quit and turned around and went back?"

Poudlum thought about this for a moment before he said, "Not him, not the way that man paddled. He could be right back there behind us just resting and listening like we are."

That thought was enough to get us up and off like the wind. The only trouble was we had left our shoes in the sinking boat and eventually our feet were getting tender. When we crossed a good-sized clearing, we stopped again, and this time, we had the advantage of being able to see a good way behind us.

After we had caught our breath, Poudlum said, "We can't keep on running blind like this. I done jammed a toe."

"Yeah, and I stepped on a sharp rock," I said as I rubbed the ball of my left foot.

"I think we been running in a pretty straight line away from the river," Poudlum speculated.

"Yeah," I agreed. "That would make us going east. At some point we got to turn left and head north if we want to get up to the bridge at Jackson."

"I've heard tell they is some bad swamps up that way. I shore don't relish the idea of going through them, 'specially without no shoes."

"Me, neither," I said. "We could keep going east, and sooner or later we ought to come out on the highway."

"Yeah, but how far you think that is?"

"I don't know, Poudlum. It could be a long way."

"Yeah, and they could be some swamps that way, too, and you know the worst part?"

"What?"

"We left them biscuits we took from Silas in the boat, and I shore am hungry. Remember, the Klan men made us lose our hushpuppies up at the ferry. Just because of the Klan, a Chinese slaver, and river rats like Silas and Dudley, we gonna starve to death."

The mention of Dudley kind of made me cringe and feel sorry for him. I told Poudlum, "I wish we hadn't of left old Dudley all trussed up like we did. When Mr. Kim went into the cabin and saw us gone, all he had to do was slit his throat like he was just a hog."

Poudlum shuddered as he said, "Maybe he didn't do that. But it's for sure he's after us, and here we sit with sore feet, hungry, thirsty, and half lost. So what we gonna do, head for the swamps or stay straight on?"

"I got an idea," I said.

Poudlum's head snapped up, and his eyes grew large as he said, "What you got in mind?"

"If we keep going, through the swamp or through the woods, our feet are just gonna get worse, and we could even get lost. Besides that, we ain't got nothing to eat or drink, and we don't even know if we could get through the woods before dark."

"So what's the idea you got?"

"We got to get back to the river."

"Back to the river? How in the world we gonna do that with a murdering slaver between us and the water?"

"We'll go around him," I said as I searched the far edge of the clearing for any movement. "Instead of running hard, we'll have to move real quiet until we know we're behind him."

"Then what?"

"Then we'll run like heck back to the river and take his boat?"

"Now you talking!" Poudlum said.

We started working our way around the big clearing,

slowly and quietly, staying inside the tree line, while we kept a sharp eye on the spot on the far side we had emerged from.

We were about two-thirds of the way around it when we saw him. Mr. Kim came out into the clearing, bent low, searching for our tracks.

I figured we had left a clean trail in the woods, what with us running with abandon the way we had, but he was having a difficult time finding a trail over the open ground.

"When he gets inside the woods on the other side, it won't take him long to figure out what we done," Poudlum whispered.

"We'll start moving again soon as he disappears into the woods," I whispered back.

When that happened, we carefully completed circling around the clearing until we reached our original trail, where we began walking softly back toward the river.

Just before we thought it was safe to start running again, Poudlum offered up what I thought was some good advice. "I don't think we ought to run full out at first. Maybe save ourselves in case we have to really run for it later."

"Yeah," I agreed. "And we can't stop till we get to that boat."

It was easy to follow the way we had come, except it wasn't in fast motion this time. We constantly cast cautious glances over our shoulders as we loped along at about three-quarter speed.

We proceeded this way for quite a spell and figured we were about halfway back when we passed the cottonwood tree where we had rested earlier.

That was when we heard the loud shriek behinds. "Stop! You stop!"

We didn't have to guess to know who it was, and it was close enough to scare us back to running wide open.

Once again, the trees swept by as I sucked air into my tortured lungs. But I knew I had some more hard running in me, and was grateful we had taken Poudlum's advice.

The pain of my bruised foot was forgotten as I made long leaps over fallen logs.

Poudlum, at my side, called out, "If he catches up with us, you go right, and I'll go left. That way he won't get us both!"

I didn't know how he had the breath to talk, so I nodded agreement to him and kept running hard, and was thankful again for Poudlum's foresight in advising us to save ourselves in case we needed to have something extra toward the end. If we hadn't we surely would have been overtaken by the mad Chinese man.

And now, in spite of the burning deep inside my chest, we seemed to be leaving our pursuer farther and farther behind. Every time I glanced backwards, I couldn't see any sign of him through the woods and couldn't hear any sounds of him.

"Maybe he give up!" Poudlum called out.

"Maybe," I gasped. "But we need to keep going. It's not far now!"

We were real close now, and I spied our big beautiful oak tree just ahead, and was so happy to see it until I lost my concentration and tripped over a vine. The ground came up like a spring and slammed me in the face and multicolored lights exploded inside my head.

By the time I got to my knees, Poudlum was kneeling beside me, breathing hard. "You all right?" he asked as he glanced nervously back behind us.

"I think so. It just knocked me dizzy."

"Can you get up?"

"In just a minute," I said as I tried to clear my head.

"If you can't, tell me, and I'll carry you 'cause we don't need to keep piddling around here."

"You think we left him?"

"For a little while, but he won't quit, and he could come busting through them bushes any time now," Poudlum said as he pulled me to my feet.

With his help, we made it over to the big tree, where I leaned up against the giant trunk of it trying to get my senses back.

What cleared my mind was a swishing sound, a flash of something spinning in the air, and the sudden thud as Mr. Kim's murderous blade struck the trunk of the tree, where it stuck and stood vibrating with a low humming sound an inch from my head.

It not only cleared my mind, but also sent us dashing like the wind for the river's edge. We crashed into the underbrush, and there was his boat, our chariot to safety. As we flung ourselves into it. Poudlum snatched the tie rope loose and pushed us off.

I was still slightly dazed, and Poudlum had to encourage me. "Grab a paddle and pull! He'll be coming at us any second now!"

Poudlum's words proved true a split-second later as

Mr. Kim burst from the bushes and dove straight into the water.

He had retrieved his weapon, and as we stared in horror, he stood waist deep in the water and once more launched his wicked blade at us.

I saw the flash of the sun's reflection on the long steel shaft as it came twirling straight toward us.

Chapter 16

The Bridge

Poudlum and I dived for the bottom of the boat just before Mr. Kim's knife split the air between us and stuck in one of the paddles leaning against the side of the boat where Poudlum had dropped it.

We looked back from our prone positions and saw it stuck in the paddle, quivering like a leaf in a strong wind.

For just a moment, we were frozen there gazing at the dagger of death which had come so close to finding its target. Then I heard splashing sounds and peeked over the side of the boat. I just about jumped out of my skin because I was eyeball to eyeball with Mr. Kim!

His hand was reaching out and was within inches of the rail of the boat. Then I felt us move away from him slightly. I looked back and saw that Poudlum had extracted the knife and was putting the paddle to use.

"Come on and help me!" he yelled.

The last thing I saw in Mr. Kim's eyes was what I perceived to be a look of panic. I supposed it was because he realized we were getting away, and he had no means left of stopping us.

To make sure his feelings were accurate, I snatched up

a paddle and helped move the boat away from him.

He was a good swimmer, and he stayed with us for a while although we kept widening the gap.

"That man can swim just as good as he can paddle," Poudlum observed. "You think he gonna swim all the way to Jackson?"

"Can't nobody swim that far, Poudlum. But I do have to say they ain't no quit in that man."

In about twenty minutes, he was a good fifty yards behind us, but he just kept coming. Pretty soon he was just a dot on the horizon, and we took a break from paddling when we saw him turn and head toward the riverbank.

"Looks like he's finally giving up," I said.

"I doubt that," Poudlum said.

"Why you say that?"

"'Cause not only are we witnesses to his act of murder, we also got the murder weapon." Poudlum said as he picked up the long knife from the bottom of the boat.

"What else can he do?"

"He could travel along the riverbank by foot and try to catch us," Poudlum told me.

I thought about that and told Poudlum I thought he would probably hightail it back down to Mobile and take one of them boats to China himself. But just in case, we started paddling again.

After a while, Poudlum started rummaging around in the bottom of the boat and came up with two cans of beans. We opened one with a pocket knife and shared it. We wanted to eat the other one but forced ourselves to save it for later.

"Shore would like to have a proper meal," Poudlum said as he polished off his share of the beans. "How far you 'spect it is up to the bridge in Jackson?"

"Can't be too much further. We ought to make it before nightfall."

"You reckon Mr. Curvin gonna be there?"

"He's probably been there since yesterday. And I bet there's folks out looking for us."

"Yeah, but they won't be looking down below the bridge. They'll be looking up above it towards Coffeeville."

"Then let's get to paddling and get on up to that bridge," I told Poudlum.

"What if ain't nobody there when we get there?"

"Then we'll just walk on up to Grove Hill."

We labored hard over the paddles, but when the sun dropped below the trees on the left bank, there was still no sign of the bridge. Twilight came and then darkness descended upon us.

"I guess that storm blew us a lot farther downriver than we thought," Poudlum lamented.

We paddled in darkness for a while, using the dark outlines of the banks of the river to stay in the middle of it. Finally the moon came up, and it wasn't quite so dark and dreary out on the river anymore. We no longer paddled with intensity, just steadily and smoothly.

"Kind of nice and peaceful out here right now," Poudlum said softly. "This is about the first time during this whole trip we ain't been rushing after catfish, running from the Klan, being captured by bootleggers, or chased by a murdering slaver."

"And yet here we are, safe and sound," I told him.

"Still powerful hungry and thirsty though."

"We won't be much longer."

"What you talking about? All we got between us and starvation is a can of beans."

"Look up yonder," I told him, pointing upriver with my paddle.

It was a ways up there yet, but there it was, soaring in a beautiful arch, high above the river. It was the bridge over the Tombigbee at Jackson.

"Praise the Lord!" Poudlum said. "There she is, and a right beautiful sight she is, too."

I thought the same thing, and wished I was an artist so I could paint the way the moonlight danced across and through the steel girders of the structure as it loomed over a stream of silver, bordered on each side by dark mansions of forests.

While I was concentrating on the bridge, I noticed a flickering dot of light under the bridge's abutment on the east side.

"Look over yonder, Poudlum! You see that light?"

"Uh-huh, I see it, and I believe it's a fire."

"I believe you are right. Let's ease over that way and see whose fire it is."

"All right," Poudlum agreed. "But let's go slow and easy and not let 'em know we here till we see who lit that blaze. It could be the Klan or that murdering Mr. Kim."

"Not likely," I told him. "But we'll still approach 'em with care."

We got close enough so we could see the flickering reflection of the fire out on the water. That's when we heard somebody say, "I'll guarantee you them boys gonna show up sooner or later."

"Well, bless my soul," Poudlum said. "I do believe that is Mr. Curvin."

"It sure is," I reassured him. "I think we gonna be all right now. But before we show ourselves, we got to decide what we gonna do."

"Do about what?"

"About what we've seen concerning the Klan and the murder, what we gonna say, and who we'll be saying it to."

Just minutes later, we paddled into the light of the fire, knowing exactly what we were going to do.

My uncle and several others had their backs to the water, facing their fire, and they were all startled when I called out across the water, "Hey, Uncle Curvin!"

He hobbled down to the river's edge, looked out at us like he couldn't believe his eyes, and said, "Praise be to the Lord, it's y'all! It's Poudlum and Ted, everybody!" he shouted back over his shoulder. "Are y'all all right? Paddle on in here, boys!"

When the bow of the boat slid up on the muddy shore, eager hands reached out to help us off the boat. Someone said, "Come on up to the fire so we can see you good, boys."

Once there, my uncle looked us up and down, and felt our arms and shoulders before he said, "Why, y'all don't seem no worse for the wear."

"We powerful hungry," Poudlum said.

"Figured you would be," Uncle Curvin said. "They's a big sack of ham and biscuits over here. Y'all sit down on this here log and eat all you want. They's a jug of fresh water here, too."

While Poudlum and I were moaning and rolling our eyes at each other as we devoured the biscuits and ham, Uncle Curvin dispatched two men to go up the river and alert everyone we were okay.

After they left in a motorboat with lights, my uncle said, "Y'all's folks are up at the ferry in Coffeeville. We been going up and down the river between here and there all day long looking for you boys, but nobody could find no sign of you."

"That's because we were down the river," I told him as I finished off another biscuit.

"Yeah, way down the river," Poudlum added.

"Down the river? Y'all mean below Jackson, down toward Mobile?"

"Yes, sir," I told him.

"What y'all doing down that way? Henry told me you was gonna meet me here."

"We started out doing that, but we got caught up in the flood water after that big rain," I told him.

Poudlum continued while I bit into another biscuit. "That's right, Mr. Curvin. Then it got dark on us, I mean pitch black, and this big old river just had its way with us, and the next thing we knew, we woke up in the top of a fallen-down tree top yesterday morning."

He gave us a toothless grin as we grinned back at him, just before he moved off to thank and disperse his friends.

I heard him instruct the men to tell mine and Poudlum's folks that we were all right and we would all sleep at my house tonight.

In a few minutes there was no one left under the bridge except the three of us, and the fire was getting dim. Poudlum and I looked at each other and nervously eyed the tree line down the river. It was comforting to have my uncle with us, but we both knew he wouldn't be a match for Mr. Kim.

"Let's get on out of here," I told Poudlum.

"Sounds good, but we ought to take the boat."

"How come?"

"If he does make it here through the woods, we don't want to leave him a ride down the river to Mobile."

Poudlum was right of course, plus I figured Mr. Kim owed us a boat because we could have saved ours if not for him.

"We can get it later," Uncle Curvin said when I told him we wanted to take the boat.

"No, sir, if you don't mind, we would like to take it tonight."

"All right then. Let's load her up on the back of the truck."

We dragged and heaved and finally slid the boat on the back of my uncle's truck. When we finished, I noticed him shining his flashlight up and down the boat.

"Wait a minute, boys, I don't believe this is my boat. Why, I know it's not because it's a good two feet longer."

"Uh, we made a trade down the river, Mr. Curvin," Poudlum told him.

"Well, did you have to give anything to boot? If not, it looks like you made a good trade."

"Can we just please get out of here, Uncle Curvin?" I said.

"Yes, sir, we ready to get away from this river, Mr. Curvin," Poudlum added.

"All right then, boys. Y'all hop in the truck."

Poudlum and I watched the dark edge of the woods until the truck got up to the main road, and we breathed huge sighs of relief when my uncle shifted into first gear and we headed up Highway 43 toward Grove Hill.

Uncle Curvin broke the silence when he said, "Henry told me about the trouble you boys run into. Y'all want to talk to me about it?"

"You ain't told nobody else, have you?" I asked.

"Naw, I didn't want y'all's folks upset anymore than they was. Besides, we got to be careful in matters concerning the Klan. I think I can square things with them boys for y'all if we plan real careful."

Neither Poudlum nor I said a word.

"So, do y'all want to tell me about what happened?"

"Not now," I told him. "We just too tired."

With that, we both settled down in the seat pretending we were going to sleep. Then pretense turned into reality, and we descended into a deep sleep, feeling safe and warm for the first time in a while.

Uncle Curvin and Poudlum stayed at my house that night. My uncle got my bed, and my mother made Poudlum and me a pallet on the floor.

We woke up to wonderful, mouthwatering aromas coming from the kitchen. Poudlum poked me and in a gravelly morning voice said, "You smell that?"

After breakfast, everybody went off to work, that is after we listened to lectures on "staying off that river."

Uncle Curvin, Poudlum, and I were sitting out on the front porch while my uncle was sipping on his third cup of coffee. We were sharpening our pocket knives, and we cast a glance at each other, knowing what was coming.

After a loud sip from his coffee cup, Uncle Curvin said, "Boys, I intend to intercede on your behalf with the Klan, but first I got to know the details of what happened."

We remained silent and just kept scraping the blades of our knives on the whetrocks.

"Well," he said. "Y'all got anything to say?"

I looked up at him and said, "We want to go see our lawyer."

Chapter 17

Telling Secrets

My uncle just about choked on his coffee. When he recovered, he said, "Y'all want to do what?"

"We want you to take us to see our lawyer," I repeated.

He leaned forward in his rocking chair, set his coffee cup on the porch rail, and said, "You talking about Mr. Alfred Jackson?"

"Yep, he's our lawyer," Poudlum confirmed.

"Wh-wh-why?" Uncle Curvin stuttered. "Mr. Jackson is an important and busy man. I'm not sure he'll drop what he's doing and talk to you boys."

"He will," I told him.

"And what makes you so sure about that?"

"After he invested our reward money from the bank, he told us if we ever needed his help to call on him anytime."

"That's exactly what he said," Poudlum added.

I could tell my uncle was tossing all this around in his head because he got quiet for a few moments. Then he said, real serious-like, "This is something that's real important to you boys?"

"Yes, sir." I told him. "It ain't just the Klan. It's also about something that happened down the river. And I ain't talking no more about it till we get to see Mr. Jackson."

He got up from the rocking chair and paced across the porch a few times while he thought about what we had said, "All right, y'all get in the truck."

When we had parked outside of Mr. Jackson's office, my uncle got out of his truck and said, "Y'all wait here while I go tell Mr. Jackson y'all want to see him."

We watched him limp up the stairs on the side of the Bank of Grove Hill, which led up to Mr. Jackson's office on the second floor. We kept our gaze on the little landing at the top of the stairs, and he hadn't been in there hardly any time before he reappeared on the landing and waved for us to come on up.

"Told him," Poudlum said.

Mr. Jackson had a large room adjacent to his office with a big round table in it surrounded by polished chairs with leather seats. He called it his conference room.

He motioned us toward it and said, "You fellows take a seat. Now, do you boys want Mr. Curvin to sit in with us, or is this going to be strictly a meeting between us?"

"Uh, yes, sir. I think it would be all right for him to be here."

He looked at Poudlum, who said, "That's fine by me, too."

"Very good," he said as he also waved my uncle into the conference room.

When we were all seated, Mr. Jackson placed a pad of paper and some pencils in front of him, looked up and said,

"Mr. Curvin seems to think you boys have had a troubling experience in the past few days down on the river. You want to tell me about it? Just start at the beginning and when one of you gets tired of talking, then let the other one take over."

I started out about how we had walked down to the river and ended up camping that night at the mouth of the Satilfa and how we had caught a boatload of catfish.

"I'll have to remember that spot next time I go fishing," Mr. Jackson said. "Go on, what happened next?"

I related how we spied the Klan men going up the creek and how we had followed them and snuck through the woods and saw the Exalted Cyclops unmask himself.

"Wait a minute, son," Mr. Jackson said. "Are you telling me y'all saw the leader of the Klan reveal his identity?"

"Yes, sir, we surely did."

"Have you related this information to anyone else?

"No, sir, we didn't because we wanted your advice before we did, or if we should."

Mr. Jackson seemed lost in thought for a moment or two. Then he said, "Do y'all know of any reason why you shouldn't reveal his identity?"

I was about talked out so I motioned for Poudlum to take over, who said, "No, sir, but we don't know of any reason why we should, either. They chased us up and down the river and who knows what they would have done to us if they had caught us."

Mr. Jackson took the time to tell Poudlum that he could tell that his new principal was going to make his mark at his school. Then he said, "The Klan knows who you boys are, so why shouldn't we know who they are?"

Mr. Jackson had a way of putting things in perspective. Poudlum looked at me, I nodded, and he blurted out, "It was the Judge! It was Judge Garrison!"

Mr. Jackson's pencil froze in his hand, and his eyes, above the glasses perched on the tip of his nose, flicked back and forth between Poudlum and me. My uncle's eyes bugged out like those of a startled squirrel.

Mr. Jackson's eyes finally rested on me, and he said, "Both of y'all real sure about that?"

"Yes, sir," I told him. "We remember him from the trial of the bank robbers."

He sighed deeply and said, "I wonder why that doesn't surprise me. Did you boys get a look at any more faces?"

"No, sir," Poudlum continued. "It was right after that when one of them snuck up on us, and we almost got caught."

"That would have been the Klexter," Uncle Curvin interjected.

Mr. Jackson jerked around to face my uncle and said, "The what?"

"The Klexter. He's the one who circles the outer area of a meeting looking for any interlopers."

Mr. Jackson turned back to Poudlum and said, "Did he get a clear look at y'all?"

"No, sir, but several folks had seen us coming to the river so it didn't take them long to figure out it was us."

"How do you know they figured out it was y'all?"

"They came to our camp two times, and we figured out they thought somebody had sent us to spy on them."

"Was it the same ones both times?"

"No, sir, the first time it was Herman Finney and his daddy."

"What happened?"

"We lied, told them we hadn't been doing nothing but fishing. We felt like we could get away with it because we left our camp at the mouth of the Satilfa in the middle of the night, paddled up the river past the ferry and made camp up there, like we had been there all night."

"What happened next?"

"While Ted was telling them all that, I eased down to the bank, and loosened the plug on their boat."

"And?"

"And Mr. Henry told us later that the boat had sunk, motor and all, and they had to swim for it."

Mr. Jackson stifled a chuckle, looked at my uncle and said, "You hear that, Mr. Curvin? They sunk the boat, motor and all."

He turned back to us and said, "You mentioned they came to your camp two times."

Poudlum gave me a look, and I took over. "Yes, sir, but the second time we didn't talk to them. Mr. Finney and the Night Hawk was at our camp when we approached it at night, and we held back and listened to them."

"The Night Hawk, you say?"

"Yes, sir."

"But you didn't see anyone else unmasked at the meeting. How did you know he was this person you call the Night Hawk?"

"It was on account of his boots."

"How's that?'

"We saw his boots under his robe at the Klan meeting, and they had silver toes on them. And the man with Mr. Finney standing by the fire at our camp had those same boots on."

"Why do they call him the Night Hawk?"

"Uh," my uncle interjected again, "he's the one who conducts new members through the ceremony."

Mr. Jackson paused, looked inquiringly over the top of his glasses at my uncle, and said, "Are you familiar with all the titles of Klan members, Mr. Curvin?"

"Well, uh, most of them," he confirmed.

"Do you mind if I ask how you came into possession of such knowledge?"

"No, sir, I don't mind. People talk, and I make it my business to know things, and besides, they ain't as secret as they claim to be and would like to be."

Mr. Jackson took off his glasses, turned directly to face my uncle and said, "Are you sympathetic with their cause?"

"I make it a policy to mind my own business," Uncle Curvin answered. "But when anybody starts messing with these here two boys, I don't care who they are. They ain't no friends of mine."

"I'm glad to hear that," Mr. Jackson said as he replaced his glasses and turned back to us and said, "Now, boys, tell us who the Night Hawk is."

I swallowed hard and thought about it for a moment or two, but I trusted Mr. Jackson's judgment, and I knew Poudlum did, too, so I just said it.

"He's the county solicitor, Mr. Danny Pierce."

Mr. Jackson tossed his pencil down on the conference table and shook his head back and forth as he speculated, "My God, is the entire court system members of the Klan?"

Uncle Curvin showed no emotion at my revelation.

We went on to tell Mr. Jackson and Uncle Curvin about our catfish dinner with Mr. Henry and his wife and how we had been run out of the quarter in the middle of the night by the Klan.

"Despicable behavior!" Mr. Jackson said.

We went on to recount the events of having to hide under the ferry when the men left the two boats they intended to use to search for us the next morning, and how we had taken them down to our camp at the mouth of the Satilfa, set them on fire, and sunk them.

"Good Lord," my uncle said with a toothless grin. "That makes three boats y'all done sunk. If y'all had been out on the river much longer, they wouldn't be no boats left on it."

"We did sink one more," Poudlum volunteered.

"Huh?" Uncle Curvin said in wonder.

"Yes, sir, we sunk your boat later on. The one we had when you picked us up belonged to two bootleggers and a murdering slaver."

When Poudlum said that, I thought my uncle's and Mr. Jackson's jaws would drop off as they stared at us in disbelief.

Mr. Jackson recovered first and said, "I take it this situation you're referring to now didn't involve the Klan?"

I took it upon myself to clear up the confusion. "No,

sir, it didn't. After we set them two Klan boats on fire and sunk them, we intended to paddle on down to the bridge at Jackson and meet Uncle Curvin the next morning, like Mr. Henry had advised us to do."

I looked at Poudlum for some help, and he didn't miss a beat. "But that night and the next day it rained cats and dogs for what seemed like forever."

"Yeah, that storm and the aftereffects is what kept me over in Choctaw County longer than I had planned," Uncle Curvin interjected.

Poudlum continued, "Well, the rain finally let up, and we loaded up the boat about dark to paddle on down to Jackson and meet Mr. Curvin. But when we got out on the water, we found out the river was swelled up like a dog tick, and it just grabbed us and took us downstream with it.

"We was at the mercy of the flooded river, and we finally give up trying to use our paddles and let it take us. And it took us all right! It took us way on down the river past Jackson, and we woke up the next morning lodged in a tree top that had fell into the river. That's when Silas, the bootlegger, pulled us out and him and Dudley locked us up in a room full of whiskey with no windows."

"Slow down," Mr. Jackson said. "Why did they lock y'all up?"

"Because they wanted to sell us down the river to Mr. Kim for two hundred dollars, who was gonna take us down to Mobile and put us on a big ship to China to serve as cabin boys. Sounded like being sold as slaves to us."

"Now hold on, Poudlum," Uncle Curvin said. "You sure

you boys ain't making up a little bit of a yarn about boot-leggers and slavers?"

Mr. Jackson held his hand up with the palm out to my uncle, indicating he was interested in hearing more from Poudlum. Then he said, "There has recently been a great deal of alarm down around Mobile about young boys disappearing. This could have something to do with that. What happened after they locked you boys up?"

"We whittled our way out," Poudlum continued. "Took a long time, and we wore some blisters on our hands doing it, but we cut right through the floor with our pocket knives and got out that way just before Silas and Dudley busted down the door that we had stacked the boxes of whiskey against."

I could tell Poudlum had grown weary, so I picked up the story from him and told how we had been recaptured when we first encountered Mr. Kim, along with Silas in a motorboat.

"How did you know this Kim was Chinese?" Mr. Jackson asked. "Did he just look that way?"

"Yes, sir, plus he had a long skinny moustache, wore a strange black shirt, and had his hair plaited into one long pigtail down the middle of his back."

"I assume you boys escaped again?"

"Yes, sir, while Silas and Mr. Kim went to make a last whiskey run before taking us down the river, Poudlum tricked Dudley, and then we overpowered him after Poudlum tossed some ground-up hot and dry pepper in his face."

"Where in the world did he get hot pepper flakes?"

"He keeps it in a little snuff can and he was pretending to get himself a dip, but instead of doing that, he tossed the pepper in Dudley's face."

"And did that incapacitate him?" Mr. Jackson asked.

I wasn't exactly sure what that word meant, but I had an idea so I said, "He fell down on the floor blinded, choking, and gagging."

"May I ask how Poudlum came into possession of a snuff can full of ground-up hot pepper?"

"Why, he keeps one in his pocket."

"Whatever for?"

"Well, mostly in case we run up on a bad dog, which we have been known to do. However, in this case it worked on a bad bootlegger."

Chapter 18

Evidence Revealed

"I must say you boys are a resourceful duo," Mr. Jackson quipped. "So, y'all were able to escape again before Silas and Mr. Kim got back from their whiskey run?"

"Well, sort of," I told him. Then I turned toward Poudlum and asked if he wanted to tell what happened.

"Uh-uh," he said with a fear-shiver. "I don't even want to think about it. You go ahead and tell."

I wasn't too excited about recounting that story either, but it had to be done, so I set about it. I told how we stayed up that tree till dawn when Silas and Mr. Kim came back.

When I uttered the part where Mr. Kim had struck Silas down with his murderous blade, Mr. Jackson dropped his pencil, gasped and said, "Are you saying he murdered the man?"

"That's right. He did," Poudlum interjected.

Uncle Curvin's eyes were about the size of a couple of saucers when he said, "Boys, it can't get no worse than accusing somebody of murder. Are you sure he was dead?"

"He was laying there dead as a hammer," Poudlum declared. "You would have been, too, if you had been stuck with that long blade."

Mr. Jackson regained his composure and said, "Why do you think he killed Silas?"

"Probably 'cause he wanted to just take us and not pay Silas and Dudley their two hundred dollars."

As he picked up his pencil and resumed writing, Mr. Jackson said, "What did Kim do then?"

"He went on up and into the cabin where I 'spec he probably cut poor old Dudley's throat."

I could see the pity for Dudley in Poudlum's eyes and hear it in his voice, too. And I could feel his pain because we knew we had left him tied up and unable to defend himself.

Poudlum confirmed my thoughts when he said, "Old Dudley wasn't too smart, but he did make some good biscuits."

"It's a good thing Kim never knew you boys were witnesses to his dastardly deed," Uncle Curvin said.

Poudlum cast a look at me and wordlessly gave me the floor.

"Uh, that's the problem we have. He does know we saw him."

"Oh, Lord have mercy!" Uncle Curvin moaned. "I thought y'all was hid up the tree."

"We was, but the minute he went into the cabin, we skedaddled out of that tree, jumped into our boat, and started paddling hard."

"But he had a motorboat to catch y'all with," Mr. Jackson observed.

"We took the time to disable his motor before we took off," I told him.

He rolled his eyes and said, "I should have known that."

Mr. Jackson seemed to be talking to himself as he wrote. "He's probably already done away with the bodies. Too bad we don't have any other evidence."

Poudlum reached inside his shirt, pulled out a bundle and rolled it out on the table. "How about this?" he said, as the murder weapon tumbled to the center of the conference table.

I thought my uncle and Mr. Jackson were both going to have some kind of conniption fit they made such a to-do over Mr. Kim's knife. When they finally collected themselves, my uncle leaned in close and said, "I believe I see some little specks of blood on the blade!"

"Don't nobody touch it!" Mr. Jackson said as he jumped up and dashed out of the room.

He was back in a flash with a big brown envelope, which he wrote something on. Then he picked up the knife with his handkerchief and placed it inside the envelope.

We silently watched as he went over and began working the combination of a steel safe against the wall. After he opened the thick metal door, he deposited the envelope into the safe. Before he closed the door, I noticed he took a pistol out of the safe and slid it inside his coat. Afterwards he returned to his seat at the table, took up his pencil again and said, "Now, how is it you boys think he knows you witnessed the murder?'

Poudlum took up the story and said, "Because he come

tearing out of that cabin while we was paddling off. He jumped in his boat, and when he figured out we had ruined his motor, he started paddling after us.

"It was all we could do, with both of us paddling, to stay ahead of him. I never seen a man who could paddle, run, and swim like he could."

"Go on," Mr. Jackson encouraged Poudlum.

"By paddling with all we had, we managed to stay ahead of him, that is until our boat started sinking. That's right, we sunk another boat, but this time it was ours. We managed to get to shore just before she went under, and that's when the footrace started."

"He chased you?"

"He chased us through the woods like a crazy man. We finally circled back on him and was getting away in his boat when he come tearing out of the woods and threw that knife at us. That's how we got it. We ducked and it stuck in a paddle on the boat."

Poudlum sounded plum tuckered out just from telling about the chase, so I finished up.

"He even took to chasing us in the water. He started swimming and stayed behind us for a while, but he finally give up, and the last we saw of him was when he went back ashore. But he was still on the east side of the river so we figured he might come on up through the woods chasing us. After that, we paddled hard and finally got on up to the bridge at Jackson where we found Uncle Curvin and them."

"I imagine you boys were mighty proud to see those folks," Mr. Jackson said.

"Yes, sir, we was proud as punch," I answered.

Mr. Jackson straightened up his papers, stood up from the table and said, "You boys just relax for a few minutes. Mr. Curvin, would you step over to my office with me?"

After they left the room, Poudlum and I sat there nearly as exhausted from telling our story as we had been when it really happened.

"What you think they talking about?" Poudlum asked.

About that time I saw motion through the window and upon closely observing, I saw it was Uncle Curvin and Mr. Jackson standing on the landing outside the entrance to his office. I also noticed the window was slightly cracked.

"Come on and we'll see," I told Poudlum as I started scooting across the floor, staying low so I wouldn't be seen. Poudlum followed, and soon we were scrunched down below the windowsill with our ears cocked to the opening.

We picked up Mr. Jackson's voice in mid-sentence, "—and I want you to hightail it down to Mobile and deliver this envelope. Don't waste any time. I'm sure you realize how extremely important this matter is."

We peeked up over the edge of the windowsill and saw my uncle take the envelope and heard him say, "Don't you be fretting about it, Mr. Jackson. I'll take care of everything and report back to you tonight."

As they were saying their goodbyes, we scooted back over to the table and had barely reclaimed our seats when Mr. Jackson came back into the room.

I knew something was up by the look on his face. He sat down across from us at the table and began to speak.

"I know you boys have been through a lot in the last few days, but instead of going home, and in the interest of your safety, would it be all right if the two of you stayed with me a couple of days?"

Poudlum and I immediately turned our heads to look at each other, but despite our ability to sometimes transfer information without speaking, we were both drawing a blank as to the reason for Mr. Jackson's request.

So I turned back to him and asked, "Sir, what do you mean by saying in the interest of our safety? Safety from what?"

"It's like this, boys. I don't think we have anything to be concerned about from the Klan. Oh, they might threaten and intimidate you, but I don't think they would physically harm you."

"Then how come they do like they do, Mr. Jackson?" Poudlum asked.

"That's a complicated question, son. But basically I think it's because it's very difficult for human beings to get over their differences. It seems like we want everyone around us to be just like we are. And I'm afraid it will take a lot of time and work to get over that, but when I see and talk to you two young fellows, I believe there is hope."

My thoughts were whirling, but I had his concern for our safety narrowed down. He was worried about Mr. Kim! "Mr. Jackson," I said in a shaky voice, "you don't think—"

"Now no need to get flustered," he said to calm me.

"You think that murdering slaver is gonna come all the way up here to get us?" Poudlum moaned as his eyes grew large.

"No, I don't," Mr. Jackson said. "But you never know what these types will do, so I think we ought to take proper precautions. That's why I asked if you boys would like to stay under my care until I can get the matter cleared up."

"How do you plan to do that?" I asked.

He stroked his chin whiskers as if in thought before he said, "As far as the Klan is concerned, I plan to write an editorial in the newspaper and expose the identity of the judge and the solicitor. That way, they should be satisfied as to the question of whom you boys were working for when you spied on them."

"But wait," Poudlum said with a puzzled look on his face. "We really wasn't doing that."

"That's of no matter," Mr. Jackson replied. "By using that strategy, it will eliminate any reason for them to be concerned with you boys anymore."

Poudlum and I looked at each other again, and this time we knew we both were thinking what a smart man Mr. Jackson was. But thinking further about what he had just said made me feel concern for him, so I asked, "But then wouldn't the Klan come after you?"

His eyes twinkled, and he smiled for the first time since I could remember, just before he said, "I would welcome them coming after me, but I don't think they will.

"What we have to be concerned about is this Mr. Kim, if that's what his real name is. I didn't mention it while you boys were relating your story, but I was already aware of an ongoing investigation of missing boys in the area south of Jackson and on down toward Mobile.

"The encounter you boys had and the information you

have furnished may be the first break in the case, and I've sent Mr. Curvin down to alert the authorities. So you see, I would feel much better if you both remained under my protection until the culprit has been apprehended."

Poudlum and I nodded agreement simultaneously, and Mr. Jackson said, "Good, that's settled. There's no need to alarm your parents, so I'll send word that for a few days you both will be doing some chores for me, and we'll find you some so we won't be fibbing."

It was getting on toward noon so Mr. Jackson took us to a café and bought our dinner.

They didn't serve colored people in that restaurant, but when we walked in, Mr. Jackson swept his gaze across the big room as if daring somebody to say something about us having Poudlum with us. It seemed nobody wanted to, and it was the kind of food we had been hankering for—fried chicken with creamed potatoes and gravy, along with some early peas, cornbread, and sweet tea.

Mr. Jackson smiled, and as we cleaned our plates, he said, "You boys eat like you got a hollow leg."

"That was mighty tasty, just what we been wishing for, and we surely do thank you," I told him.

"Yes, sir, that was mighty fine," Poudlum said as he licked his lips. "We been living off catfish for days, and there was some times in between when we was too busy running, hiding, or paddling to even stop and eat."

We whiled away the afternoon in Mr. Jackson's library. I found a copy of *Robinson Crusoe*, and Poudlum settled on *Treasure Island*.

Mr. Jackson's housekeeper fixed us another tasty meal

that night, and Poudlum and I retired to his guest bedroom, which was about the most comfortable-looking room either one of us had ever seen.

We marveled at the shiny floor and the two heavy twin beds. Later on, after we had blown the lamp out and curled up in those beds, through the window, I saw a flash of movement outside in the dark yard.

"Poudlum!" I whispered. "Did you see that?"

"What? What did you see?"

"I saw something move out there," I said. We crawled over and crouched on our knees at the window and strained our eyes, searching in the darkness.

"There it is! You see it?" Poudlum said as he grabbed my arm.

"Uh-huh," I breathed softly as I felt the fear seeping into me.

What we saw was a dark figure pass though the bushes and disappear around toward the rear of the house. He was moving and there were too many shadows to tell if it was who we dreaded it could be.

Chapter 19

Back on the River

My fear intensified when I suddenly got that feeling that someone else was in the room with us. Poudlum must have felt it too, because he began to fumble with the lock on the window. I supposed he was doing that so we could open it, dive through it, and escape.

But then we heard the kind and welcome voice of Mr. Jackson say, "Is everything all right, boys?"

"Somebody's out there!" I told him in a loud whisper as he stood framed in the doorway.

"All you saw was Claude," he said calmly.

"Who's that?"

"Claude provides security here when I think it might be in our best interest. You boys can relax and get a good night's sleep. You're safe here."

What Mr. Jackson said made us feel a lot better, and there was also something calming about the tone of his voice. We got back under the covers after that, and I was about to doze off when I heard the low sounds of Uncle Curvin's voice intermingled with Mr. Jackson's.

They were talking fast, and I couldn't quite make out the words, just that they both sounded excited and part of me wanted to go in there and see what was going on, but the other part of me was in a soft warm place, a fleeting moment from sound sleep, and that side won.

Poudlum woke me up the next morning. It was light outside, and he was shaking my shoulder.

"Hey," he said as my eyes popped open. "Did you hear them talking a lot just before we went to sleep last night?"

"I sure did," I said as I sat up in bed.

"Then why didn't you go in there and see what all the ruckus was about?"

"Why didn't you?" I answered.

"Too tired and sleepy, I guess. Come on, get dressed and let's go find out what's going on."

We dressed and rushed out but couldn't find anyone until we got to the kitchen where we found Mr. Jackson's housekeeper, Leola Hensley.

As soon as we walked into the room, she looked directly at us, pointed toward the table, and said, "Y'all sit yourselves down, and I'll stir you up something to eat."

Although we had seen her at last night's meal, we hadn't had the occasion to talk directly with her. I could tell right off that Miss Leola wasn't a woman to trifle with. Evidently, Poudlum felt the same way because he beat me to the table. And it didn't seem like it was no time before she slid steaming plates of grits, eggs, and biscuits in front of us.

While we were eating and she was turned away from us, I poked at Poudlum so he would look at me. When he did, I nodded toward Miss Leola in the hopes he would take the lead and ask her where everybody was.

He nodded okay, and when she returned to the table to refill our milk glasses, Poudlum said, "Miss Leola, would you happen to know where Mr. Jackson or Mr. Curvin might be?"

She stopped in mid-step with the pitcher of milk in her hand, looked down at us and said, "Mr. Jackson is working in his office, I suppose, like he always do." As she turned and headed back toward the ice box she added, "And it ain't my job to keep up with Curvin Murphy."

I kicked Poudlum under the table, encouraging him to pursue the conversation with her.

I could tell he was intimidated by her, just as I was, but he gathered up his courage one more time and said, "Did, maybe, Mr. Jackson leave word for us?"

"He certainly did," she said as she busied herself in front of the sink.

When she didn't say anything else, I couldn't stand it anymore, and I couldn't wait for Poudlum, so I dared to speak to her myself.

"Did he say what we ought to do, Miss Leola?"

I expected her to say he certainly did again, but she surprised me and said, "He told me to tell y'all to tend to your chores till he sends for you," with no indication of what the chores consisted of.

I looked at Poudlum, and we both rolled our eyes as I whispered, "Your turn."

We had cleaned our plates when Poudlum said, "That was a delicious breakfast, Miss Leola. I reckon we ready to get on with them chores now, if you would be kind enough to point them out to us."

I was impressed by Poudlum. He had asked her exactly what we wanted to know in a polite manner, but neither of us expected her answer.

"He say for y'all to go into his library and read some of his books."

We were both flabbergasted because we had expected the chores to consist of pulling weeds or some other form of yard work.

"He also said y'all could talk to each other some in betwixt the reading," she added.

"Uh, did he say how long?" I ventured.

"Till he sends for y'all," Miss Leola said just before she turned and disappeared through a swinging door.

"That woman's 'bout as hard to get something out of as Mr. Curvin," Poudlum told me later in the library.

We were like two tortured souls in that library, trying to read and wondering what was going on. It was just before noon when we heard the front door slam and then steps coming down the hallway.

"Hey, boys," my uncle called out. "Where y'all at?"

We rushed out to meet him and immediately bombarded him with questions.

"What did you do in Mobile? Where's Mr. Jackson?" I asked.

"And what are we supposed to do now?" Poudlum said.

"Hold your horses, boys," he said. "We got to get over to Mr. Jackson's office lickety-split. Come on, I'll tell you about things on the way."

We piled into my uncle's truck and started peppering him with more questions as he backed out of the driveway.

"They's a big manhunt going on down the river. It turned out y'all's Mr. Kim is about the most-wanted man in Alabama."

We sat slack-jawed, rapt with attention as he continued. "As soon as I delivered Mr. Jackson's information to the Mobile County Sheriff, he got on the phone and pretty soon he had every lawman from Jackson down to Mobile Bay on the case.

"What they doing is some of 'em are heading north from Mobile and another passel of 'em are heading south from Jackson with boats in the water and men and dogs along both sides of the river."

"They intend to trap Mr. Kim somewhere in between 'em," Poudlum guessed

"That's exactly what they hope to do. Now listen up boys. Y'all gonna have to tell your story again—the part after y'all got swept down the river—to some gentlemen from Mobile. They over at Mr. Jackson's place waiting on us."

"How come we got to go through it again?" I asked.

"It's because they wanting a real detailed accounting of what y'all say and a real good description of Kim. It'll be all right. They won't keep y'all for long, and then I'll take y'all for a hamburger."

My uncle was wrong. The men kept us for a very long time and made us tell our story over and over. It turned out that Mr. Kim wasn't Mr. Kim at all, but rather a man with a name so long we couldn't even pronounce it, much less spell it.

We could tell they wanted to catch him real bad by the way they would get excited and start scribbling on their pads when we thought of something new about him.

We got restless, and we were very hungry when we finally got some relief. It was when one of their assistants came rushing into the room so excited he could hardly get it out, but he finally said, "They done caught him! Chased him down in a stolen motorboat in Baldwin County!"

I never saw a group of men move so fast. They gathered up their papers and all bolted for the door at once. The one in charge poked his head back in the door and said, "We appreciate your help, boys, and we'll be in touch with y'all."

Poudlum and I just sat there by ourselves wondering what was next. That's when Mr. Jackson came into the room and sat down at the table with us.

"Well, boys," he said, "once again you can be proud of yourselves. Thanks to you the river will be rid of the scourge of Kim and his cohorts. Before long, you'll probably have to testify in court, but there's no need for concern because I'll be there with you.

"I thought y'all might also want to know that Dudley didn't get his throat cut after all. He's been captured, too, and is being very cooperative with the authorities."

I was relieved to know that our leaving Dudley tied up didn't get him murdered and I could tell Poudlum was, too, when he asked, "How in the world did he get away from Mr. Kim?"

Mr. Jackson said, "It seems he broke loose from his bonds at the same time as Silas and Kim arrived, and he witnessed the same thing as you boys did through a crack in the window, and then quickly escaped through the hole you boys had cut in the floor of the back room."

"Old Dudley wasn't as dumb as he seemed," Poudlum said with a grin.

Mr. Jackson continued, "Since you boys aren't in any kind of danger anymore, I suppose it'll be all right for you to go on home."

"Bu-bu-but, Mr. Jackson," Poudlum stuttered. "What about the Klan?"

In answer, he slid a copy of the weekly newspaper, fresh off the press, across the table toward us.

Our eyes bugged out when we saw the story on the front page. It was written by Mr. Jackson and the headline blared: Klan Leaders Exposed.

The story identified the judge and the solicitor as the Exalted Cyclops and the Night Hawk, and went on to demand their resignation from public office.

When we finished reading the story, Mr. Jackson said, "All the Klan wanted from you boys is who they thought y'all were spying on them for. Now they know what they thought they wanted to know, that it was for me, even though we know it wasn't. If they want to come after anybody, it'll be me and not you boys."

"I suppose you're right about that," I told him.

"The only thing is," Poudlum said, "the Klan, Silas and Dudley, and Mr. Kim sure did mess up a good fishing trip."

Mr. Jackson scratched his chin whiskers and said, "Maybe there's something we can do about that."

ABOUT A WEEK LATER Uncle Curvin and Poudlum picked me up at my house, and we headed toward Mr. Jackson's house.

After all the excitement had died down, Mr. Jackson had offered to let Poudlum and me take his motorboat, put it in the river at Jackson, and have ourselves a nice fishing trip all the way up to Mr. Henry's ferry in Coffeeville, where Uncle Curvin would pick us up and deliver the boat, Poudlum and me all back home.

Uncle Curvin picked the days for us by studying the *Old Farmer's Almanac*. He claimed we had two good sunny days, cool nights, and very little breeze, which would make for the perfect fishing trip.

When I saw that boat in Mr. Jackson's garage, I knew he had been having things done to it because it shined like a new apple. While I was admiring the motor at the rear of the boat, Poudlum called me from up at the front of the boat and said, "Hey, come look at this!"

When I got there, he pointed to the side of the boat and said, "A boat is supposed to have a name, and look at the one this boat's got."

There it was, printed in neat white letters on the red boat. We were going fishing in the *Night Hawk*.

The boat was also outfitted with poles, fishing gear, bait, food, water, sleeping bags, and a tent, all strapped down neatly inside it. It was just about the finest boat we had ever laid eyes on.

We helped Uncle Curvin hook up the boat trailer to the back of his truck, and we were preparing to pull out of the driveway when Miss Leola appeared extending a big brown bag through the truck window to us.

"This is for y'all to nibble on before you get the fish to frying."

When we got the boat in the water at Jackson, Uncle Curvin went out on the water with us and gave instructions and let us practice running the boat. It was a lot different than paddling because things happened much faster.

After my uncle promised to meet us in Coffeeville, he gave us a shove out into the water.

"You ready?" Poudlum asked with his hand on the starter rope.

Pretty soon we were roaring up the Tombigbee leaving a wake and all of our troubles behind us. The wind blew in our faces, and we had time to study things, not being chased or paddling around in the dark.

We didn't even go ashore that night. We just anchored the boat at the mouth of the Satilfa and fished late by the light of a lantern. Later on, we crawled into our sleeping bags while the sound of the river and the gentle rocking of the boat lulled us to sleep.

The next morning we fished some more and took us a swim in the mouth of the creek before we secured everything and headed the boat north, taking turns driving.

We sighted the ferry, and there stood Mr. Henry and Uncle Curvin on the edge of it. They had some ice to put all the fish on.

We got back to Grove Hill well before dark and backed

Mr. Jackson's boat into his garage, and the next thing I knew, I was standing in my front yard waving goodbye to Uncle Curvin and Poudlum.

They weren't even out of sight yet, and I was missing them already.

About the Author

Ted M. Dunagan was born and grew up in rural southwestern Alabama. He served in the U.S. Army, attended Georgia State University, and retired from a career in business in 2003. He received the 2009 Georgia Author of the Year Award in Young Adult Fiction for his debut novel, *A Yellow Watermelon*. The book was also named to the inaugural "25 Books All Young Georgians Should Read" list compiled by the Georgia Center for the Book. He followed his first success with a sequel, *Secret of the Satilfa*, which earned the 2011 Georgia Author of the Year Award. He lives in Monticello, Georgia, where he writes news, features, and a weekly column for the *Monticello News*.

READ MORE ADVENTURES OF
TED AND POUDLUM IN

a Yellow
WATERMELON

by TED M. DUNAGAN

"In *A Yellow Watermelon,* Ted refuses to be an observer of life in rural Alabama of 1949. He's in the middle of the action, looking and listening and thinking. He learns secrets and stirs up dangers that force him to take a courageous stand against long established customs that are unfair and dishonest. What can an 'almost twelve year old' do to make a difference? With the help of forbidden friends, Ted's inventive solutions will surprise the reader and keep the pages turning to the tasty end of the story."
— AILEEN KILGORE HENDERSON

"A fine, well-told tale of friendship between two smart, likable boys— one white, one black. Memorable [and] generous-hearted."
— *Kirkus Reviews*

ISBN 978-1-58838-197-2
240 pages • $21.95

Available from your favorite bookstore or online at
WWW.NEWSOUTHBOOKS.COM/WATERMELON